Andy:

Flying High
For
The King

By

Ronna M. Bacon

Isaiah 40:31

But those who wait on the Lord
Shall renew their strength;
They shall mount up with wings like eagles,
They shall run and not be weary,
They shall walk and not faint.

NKJV

Table of Contents

Chapter 1

The freshness of the early fall morning greeted Andrew Donovan as he walked towards the plane hangars located on land owned by the Barnabas Foundation, his employer. He was headed away from there, needing some time and a vacation. Barnabas Carey, his employer, had just looked at him and then agreed, asking how much time he wanted. Andy had shrugged, not sure how long, but he would be in touch, he promised.

Drawing in a deep breath that cleared his lungs, Andy smiled. He was off, he thought, to fly wherever it was that he felt like. It was a change for him, usually heading out wherever it was he was needed. This time? It was for him.

Andy's head turned as he heard a sound and then he shook it. No, he was the only one here at present, he thought. The mechanic had been around, helping to move the plane from the hangar and had then disappeared.

Frowning, Andy continued to work away, his pre-flight done. He paused once more, certain that he heard a noise. He spun and then circled the plane, returning to stand, his eyes on the hangar. No, he thought, there can't be anyone here.

He approached the hangar cautiously, pausing outside as he once more heard a faint noise. *Lord, I have no idea what I'm facing but You do. Protect me, please, dear Lord.*

Andy searched the hangar, not seeing anything. He paused, a hand rubbing at his face before he ran it through his auburn hair, styled just a little longer than expected. His deep blue eyes were troubled.

Heading for the open door, his steps paused and then stopped. Andy's gaze was fixed on the young woman, his age he thought, who stood just inside the open door. Her arm was tight in the grasp of a burly, older man. A gun was pointed to her head, scaring Andy, and not much did that.

"Move this way." The man's voice was harsh and rough. He jammed the gun harder at the young woman, drawing a soft cry from her.

Reluctant to comply, Andy moved slowly forward, desperately searching for a way out for them both and not seeing one.

"Move it. Or she dies."

Andy kept his eyes on the eyes of the young woman, a frown crossing his face. He could see the fear in the deep green eyes but also anger. *Lord, I have no idea what I just walked into, but You do. Help me to free her.* He took in the short cap red curls and sighed once more. *Why me, Lord? I'm supposed to be on holiday.*

"In the plane. Now, or she dies." The man's words lashed at Andy, causing him to jump.

—

"Why? You're trespassing, you know."

"Doesn't matter. You're the pilot. I've been watching you. You're flying us out of here." The gun moved to point at Andy who shuddered and then walked towards the plane.

He was followed closely by the man, the lady's reluctant steps forced from her as she was almost dragged to the plane and then up the stairs. Andy raised and locked the stairs before he turned once more.

"Where are we heading?"

"Doesn't matter right now. In there and get us up into the air." The man shoved the lady into the copilot seat and then sat behind her, his gun still evident.

Andy stared back at him before staring at the lady. He frowned as he stared at her. She looked familiar but he wasn't sure about that even.

"I need to file a flight plan. Where are we heading?" Andy stared back at the man, feeling that was all he was doing at the moment.

"File it for where you were heading. I'll tell you where I want you to go once we're in the air."

Andy ground his teeth together. This was not how it worked. Not at all. He was too careful in how he flew and with his flight plan.

Andy shifted on his seat. He had been flying in a circle, it seemed, for almost an hour. The man had simply told him to do that. Andy frowned. There was something wrong, he decided, only he had no idea what. He watched the sky, seeing clouds moving in and drew a deep breath. They were heading into a storm and that concerned him.

"We're heading into a storm." He glanced back at the man, finding the gun trained on him. "We'll need to land."

"No landing. Keep flying."

"I can't just fly into that storm." Andy heard the warnings coming across his headset. "They're warning everyone to land."

"No landing. Keep flying."

Andy was frustrated and worried. He needed to land, that much he knew, but he wasn't being allowed to. His gaze shifted to the lady, who was watching him closely. She had not spoken.

His voice low, Andy finally spoke to her.

"We're in danger in more ways that one. I would like to know your name."

She glanced back at the man, who was staring out of the window, not seeming to be paying attention to them.

"It's Oshea Flanagan. How serious are you about the weather?"

"Deadly serious. If we don't land, we'll likely crash." Andy began to feel the weather beating around his plane and struggled to keep control. "This isn't good. Brace yourself, Oshea, we're landing whether your friend wants us to or not."

"He's not my friend. I have no idea who he is."
A cry came from her as a hand slapped across her face.

"Hey!   Leave her alone!"   Andy was momentarily distracted.

That moment of distraction was all it took. The wind began to toss the plane and with a sinking heart, Andy knew that he had lost control.

"Brace yourself, Oshea. We're going down."

Andy struggled to control the plane enough to land reasonably safely. The ground rushed towards them and the tree branches that they were dropping into beat at the sides of the plane. He heard a cry from Oshea as the plane landed in a clearing and then kept rolling. Andy was desperate to stop the plane but it was out of his control. He saw the trees rushing at him, heard Oshea's cry and then nothing.

Chapter 2

The forest critters gradually crept back out, eyes wary as they studied the large object that had landed in their forest, disturbing the morning and their normal way of life. When no movement came from it, they stared at it a bit longer and then went about their normal daily business. It didn't seem to be worrisome, they thought, or dangerous.

Oshea moved slightly, grimacing with pain, as her eyes cracked open slightly and she stared around. Her hand reached for Andy, touching his shoulder and shaking him. She suddenly spun, regretting it as her head pounded with pain. The man lay still. She didn't care about him, she decided, but Andy needed her help. Her seatbelt loosened, she leaned closer to Andy, reaching for his wrist. Her head dropped with relief as she felt his pulse before she stared out of the window.

Oshea sighed. They were somewhere in the middle of nowhere, in a crashed plane, surrounded by trees. The pilot was unconscious. She turned once more for the man and felt for a pulse. It was faint and fading, she thought. *This is not good. Lord, why am I in this situation? I can't carry either man out of here.*

Dropping to the ground through her window, Oshea winced at the pain she felt. Her hand clutched at her head, willing the headache to stop pounding. She searched the area and shook her head, regretting that movement.

I have no idea where we are, Lord. The only one who does is the man who calls himself Andy. I trust him and it is not in me to trust so easily or so quickly. I know that he wanted to prevent this, but couldn't. She shivered in the wind that was gaining strength and felt the first drops of rain. *Just what we need. A rainstorm.*

She crawled back up the tree near her window and back into the cockpit. Andy had not moved and she didn't think her abductor had. She spun to stare at him once more.

Who is he, Lord? I don't have any enemies. At least, I don't think I do. He just appeared last night, grabbed me as I was heading for my car after work, and shoved me into his car. His hand never left my arm the whole time. What does he want? And will we ever find out?

Oshea moved towards the rear of the plane, searching for a first aid kit and any supplies that she could find. She had no intention of staying there. As soon as she could get Andy awake, she was leaving. Bundling her supplies into a blanket, she lowered it carefully to the ground and then turned to Andy once more.

Andy stirred, moving to lean back against his seat. His eyes opened slightly as he gazed through the windshield at the trees surrounding them. He wasn't sure where he was or even who he was. He felt a hand on his arm and then the seatbelt loosening.

Groaning as he was forced to move, Andy nodded at the soft question of could he move and go through the window. She needed him to. There was a tree outside that he could hold on to. Only he needed to move.

Oshea watched Andy as he slowly moved from his seat, concern on her face and then fear as she saw the blood on his shoulder. He was hurt and she didn't know if she could stop the bleeding. She followed him out of the plane and then with an arm around him, she picked up her bundle and moved away, her steps slow enough that Andy could manage.

Oshea searched for somewhere that they would be safe and out of the weather. The wind and rain were picking up, soaking them both. She squinted as they came to a clearing. There was a cabin, she thought, her arm tightening around Andy as he stumbled, hardly able to stay on his feet.

"Andy? Can you stay with me for a few moments? I need you to stay on your feet. Please? Andy? Please?" Her voice held the sobs that she would not release as well as the fear and worry that she was feeling.

Andy finally nodded, his face whitening even more as he worked to place one foot ahead of the other, an enormous task he thought.

Oshea reached for the cabin door, praying that it would be unlocked. It moved under her hand and she hesitated just for a brief moment before she was through the door and looking for somewhere that Andy could sit. A bunk, she thought. Just what we need. She gently shoved Andy down on it, her face contorting in sympathy as he groaned with pain. She reached to swing his feet up and then for a blanket to cover him.

Searching for water, Oshea stopped to study the cabin. *This is someone's home that I just invaded, she thought, noting the tidiness of the cabin and the comfort of the furnishings. I can't help it, can I, Lord? He needs help and I can't move him any more than I have. Just let me not have hurt him too much.* She reached for the kettle, filling it, and then staring at the stove. *I can do this, she thought. I've done it before.*

A while later, she was never sure afterwards how long it was, she set the basin of water beside the bunk. She had found a pair of scissors and knew that she needed to cut away Andy's shirt. Only if she did that, what would he wear? She would have to search through his pack that she had somehow managed to bring with her.

A sound at the door had her on her feet, a hand to her mouth to control her scream. The man who entered paused and then turned to watch her.

"You're in my cabin, young lady." His voice, though stern, was gentle.

"I know. Andy needs help. I had to find somewhere for him." She was on her knees once more, her hand reaching for the wet cloths to wipe away the blood and see how much damage had been done.

—

"Your young man? He's been injured?" The man was beside her, moving her aside so that he could take over.

"He's not my young man. And yes, he has been injured." Oshea's teeth worried at her lip. "We were in a plane crash. I had to get him away from there. Away from that man"

"I see. How be we fix up your young man and then we'll talk."

Chapter 3

His hand on the kettle, the man turned to watch Oshea. She had dropped to the floor, not caring that she had injuries that needed to be cared for, her hand on Andy's as he moved restlessly. He shook his head at the pair. *Lord, what have You led me into? I know that I'll have to backtrack and see what she meant. I thought I heard a plane earlier today but didn't think anything about it.*

"Here, young lady. On your feet and to the couch. I need to look at your injuries." He pulled her to her feet and then to the couch. "My name's Simon Crocker."

"I'm Oshea Flanagan. That's Andy Donovan. I'm sorry. I just walked into your house. We'll leave as soon as I can get Andy on his feet." Oshea didn't look at the man, her eyes on Andy instead.

"You'll not be going anywhere tonight." Simon finished his assessment, something that he had thought he had left behind when he retired as a physician. He had thought that God had heard him when he said he was done with that stuff. Apparently, God knew better. He was glad that he was here for the two.

———

"There was another man, Simon." Fear stood in Oshea's eyes and he could hear it in her voice. "He kidnapped me last night. He forced Andy to take us with him. Andy didn't want to. He wanted to land somewhere but that man wouldn't let him."

"Was he still alive?" Simon watched her closely, seeing her struggle to be honest.

"He was, but I don't think he would live for long. His pulse was really faint." She looked up at the ceiling. "I need to go back and find out if he's still alive."

"Not you, Oshea. I'll go. Did you walk in a straight line from the plane?"

"As best I could. We came in from the other side of the clearing. I had a horrible time keeping Andy on his feet."

"I reckon that you did. You did fine, Oshea. You got him to help and that's what you needed to do." Simon rose, returning with a blanket. "How be you lie down for a bit? I'll see what I can find out." He watched as she sighed, leaned around him to watch Andy, and then reluctantly laid her head down. She was asleep almost as soon as her head touched the pillow. He gave a small smile as he covered her.

He stood, torn between leaving them and staying. Compassion won out and he headed for his rain gear and his walking stick. *Lord, You'll need to lead me. I'm not sure that they did walk a straight line after all.*

Reaching the plane, Simon stood for a moment. *He did good, didn't he, Lord? He landed well. If it hadn't been for those trees, he not likely would have been injured.* Simone climbed up on the wing to the window and shone his flashlight around inside the plane. The man had disappeared. He sighed. There was no way that he could search for him tonight, that was a given. It was raining too hard and had been for a while. It was doubtful that he would even find him come morning and if the rain let up.

Simon's rain gear hit the rack it was kept on as he walked towards Andy. He stood, a hand resting against the log wall, assessing the younger man. No change, is there? I won't have much sleep tonight, that's for sure. His attention turned to Oshea, and he stood over her, a frown on his face. He knew her or knew someone who looked like her. But that lady was in his past, wasn't she? Or maybe not. He would have to be careful how he asked his questions of Oshea, but question her he would. Now Andy? He frowned. No, he didn't know the young man, but it seemed that their lives were not intertwined.

Andy's sleep was restless, his body jerking and twisting as he fought to keep the plane in the air once more, his dreams rift with the motions that had failed. His eyes flickered open and closed and his head twisted. His low moans sounded through the cabin, bringing Simon to his side. He muttered quietly, Simon bending over to hear his fear for Oshea.

Simon turned for a moment to study O'Shea across the dimly-lit cabin before he turned back to Andy. A rough hand laid on his forehead stilled

Andy's movements for a moment, but only for a moment. Simon knew that he had to quiet Andy but he didn't have any of the drugs that he would have used at one time. He could feel the fever starting and that was not what he wanted to discover. He had felt Andy's body over, finding no broken bones, but the head injury worried him as did the deep bruising.

"I don't know how he didn't break anything, Lord, other than for Your hand on him. And on that young lady. There's a story there, I know. I just don't know if they will share with me or not." Simon's head turned as he heard soft footsteps and watched as Oshea lowered herself to the floor, a hand reaching for Andy's and her other hand on his cheek. He watched closely as Andy's face turned into Oshea's hand and then his movement stilled.

They have a connection, don't they already, Lord? Heal them. Protect them. They have a story to tell and I'll need to reach out to Titus, now won't I? But what can I tell him? Simon sighed to himself and reached to draw Oshea to her feet and then back to her bed. She fought him, her desire to stay with Andy, but his hand gently and firmly kept hold of her arm. Oshea settled back down, her eyes on Andy until they grew too heavy to keep open. She slept, but not a restful, restorative sleep. Simon could see the dreams that she was fighting, her face too open in her sleep to hide anything.

Chapter 4

The sounds of the early morning wafted through the open winds on the gentle breeze. Oshea stirred, rubbing at her face, before she snuggled down once more under the covers, not quite awake. Simon watched her from where he stood at the back door and just shook his head. He turned his attention to Andy, making his way to his bedside.

Andy had been restless all night and that worried Simon. He knew that he needed to get him to help but that would be a difficult task. His car was parked down at the base of the hill and that meant a walk out to it. He had never bothered bringing the driveway up, thinking that he didn't need to. He was also worried about the man that had disappeared. Where had he gone, Simon wondered? If he was hurt as bad as Oshea had thought, then he couldn't have made his way out on his own. And if he had help, it would only be a matter of time until they searched and found his home.

Oshea roused more fully, sitting up and pushing at her curls, before she scrubbed at her face. Nightmares had plagued her over night, drawing her deeper into what, she just didn't know. Her gaze

—

landed on Andy and she was on her feet, swaying as pain hit her. Oshea watched as Simon approached, a hand out to draw her into the kitchen and to a chair.

"I need to see to Andy." She tried to rise, only to find a hand keeping her in her chair.

"No, right now, we need to get some fluids down you." Simon gave a stern look at her. "That means juice, water, broth. You will drink, Oshea, or I will not let you near Andy."

"But I need to. It's my fault he was hurt. I don't know what the man wanted. He just grabbed me two nights ago and then made Andy take us in his plane." She looked up, tears hovering in her eyes. "Why?"

"Did you know the man?" Simon sat a cup of tea in front of her, knowing that she would drink.

"No, I didn't. I don't remember seeing him before. He was just there and then I was in his car. He wouldn't let go of me. He drove around and then made his way to that hangar." She frowned at Simon. "I don't get it."

"Did you know the hangar?" Simon turned to watch Andy. He had searched through his wallet, albeit reluctantly, to find a name that he could call. Finding the name of Barnabas Carey had stopped Simon, who had frowned.

"No. It had a name on it that I recognized but I don't know why."

"The Barnabas Foundation/"

Oshea nodded. "That's it. I am not familiar with this company or why I would be taken there. Do you know?" She looked at Simon with hope in her eyes.

"No, I don't. Now, young lady, your family. Will they worry about you?" Simon's keen eyes watched closely.

Oshea shook her head. "No, they won't. I have a brother but he's not around. I have no idea where he is. My parents? They are so wrapped up in their business I hardly see them. They're never home." She blinked rapidly. "That's not life, you know."

"No, it's not. Now, about that man? I went back to the plane last night. He wasn't there."

"Not there? How can that be? I thought that he was almost dead!" Oshea sat back, horror on her face. "He'll be after me, won't he? And Andy. Oh, what will I do?"

"For now, you stay here. My place is hard to find. My cabin is hidden. God led you last night to here."

"He'd do that?" Oshea studied him and then nodded. "Of course, He would." She was on her feet and then on her knees beside Andy as he moved, moans coming from him. "Simon?"

"I know, Oshea. I need to get him into the hospital. He needs more treatment than I am prepared to give him. You landed in the home of a retired physician, you know." He grinned at her for a moment. "Now, let's see how your fellow is this morning."

"My fellow? Oh, he's not my fellow. I'm a stranger to him."

"He works for the Barnabas Foundation, Oshea. The men there are known for taking care of people, particularly ladies in distress."

"Is that what I am? A lady in distress?" Oshea stared at Simon and then at Andy, her hand reaching for Andy's, finding his closing over hers that morning. "How bad is he hurt?"

"I don't think that there are any internal injuries, Oshea, but without imaging, I can't be certain. You know, x-rays, ultrasounds, Cat scan."

"Oh, those! How do we do it then, Simon?"

"We'll have to wait until he's well enough to walk. Neither one of us can carry him out. It is a bit of a walk and down hill to my car."

"I see. Then, God will have to heal him." Oshea was on her feet, heading for the kitchen, returning with a mug of broth that Simon had ready. "Can he have this?"

"Just sips." Simon reached to hold Andy more upright as Oshea held the mug to his lips, watching as he sipped and swallowed, pain on his face. "I got some pain medication down him earlier."

"He hasn't awakened yet, though, has he? Is this what the man wanted?" Oshea sat back on her feet.

"What do you mean?" Simon set the mug aside and then pulled up a chair to sit. "Why would you say that?"

Oshea shrugged. "I don't know. It's just as if he knew Andy and wanted to harm him. He just didn't seem to be driving around aimlessly. It was as if he knew where he was going."

"He did? Then, we'll need to talk to someone. Do you know how far you are from the town Andy lives in?"

Oshea shook her head, a puzzled look on her face.

"It's not that far, only about two hours by road."

"We didn't get that far then? He had Andy flying in circles or so it seemed. Andy was worried, I could tell."

"I'm sure he was. He had a storm coming at him, you were in danger, and the man had a gun, you said. That makes for a worrying time. Now, let's see what we can do. I have some cell service, so I will call my friend, who is a police officer. He'll come out and talk with you."

"How can he do that? Won't he be followed?" Oshea began to nibble at her lower lip, worried for Simon.

"Not at all. He comes out at least once a week, just for a meal and to make sure I'm okay." Simon bowed his head and prayed for the young couple, certain that they were still in grave danger, only he didn't know who from. Not knowing meant that he couldn't help to protect them.

Chapter 5

Oshea paced the cabin. She wanted to run, to get away, to hide, to protect Andy. She spun to stare at him and then spun back to stare at the door. She could just leave, she knew. But Oshea would not do that. Not when the person who had tried to protect her and save her was unconscious. She worried about him.

Gradually making her way to the back door, she opened it and peeked out. Simon sat on the edge of his deck and turned, motioning her to come out and sit with him.

"Is this safe, Simon?"

"About as safe as it can be." He watched as she finally sat, her arms wrapping around herself.

"Did you speak with your friend?" Oshea had hopes that he had been able to but no hope that it would help.

"I did. He said he'd be up today or tomorrow. He wasn't sure which day would work. He'll help me to get your fellow from here to town."

"He will, but Andy's not my fellow." Oshea's face grew grave and then saddened. "I'll never have one of them." She didn't hear the fumbling footsteps as Andy crept across the deck.

Simon watched, ready to rise and help him, but Andy simply shook his head and then sat beside Oshea, an arm around her. Oshea jumped, her eyes huge with fear as she stared at Andy.

"You shouldn't be up, Andy. You need to be in bed. You were hurt."

"It's okay, sweetheart. It's okay. I'll go back. I just wanted to make sure that you were okay. Were you hurt?" His eyes, though blurred, watched her, thinking how beautiful she was and that he didn't want her to walk out of his life. Just like all the other men who worked for the Barnabas Foundation, he had found his lady in trouble and fell with one look.

"You're sure? You don't look too steady on your feet."

Andy simply grinned at her, his eyes meeting Simon.

"Where are we?" His voice was still rough.

"I'm Simon. Somehow or other your young lady found my cabin. I am a retired doctor so you were led to a good spot."

"I see. My plane? Do you know how damaged it is?"

"I'm no expert but you did a good job bringing it down. You'll need to bring in someone to remove it and that will be a difficult task."

"Not really. Barnabas has resources that he will call." Andy sighed, reaching for his phone. "I need to call him."

"Not right now, Andy. We need to get some nourishment into you and then you'll be ready to go back to bed." Simon was on his feet, lifting Andy to his, and then hand to Andy's back, moving him back into the cabin and to a chair.

Oshea watched, her hand holding Andy's phone, one that she had taken from him as he had raised himself up. It startled her when it vibrated and she almost dropped it. She practically ran across the kitchen, tossing it to Andy, who caught it and then grinned at her.

"Scared you, did it?"

She nodded. "It did. I didn't think it would work out here."

"It does, Oshea. Remember I told you that." Simon shook his head, his eyes on her before he frowned.

"You did. I forgot." Oshea sank into a chair, her head on her arms. "I'm just so tired, Andy. I just want to sleep."

Simon was at her side, a hand out to lift her head. The whiteness of her face worried him.

"Simon? She's hurt?" Andy was on his feet, hands planted on the table, his gaze shifting between Oshea and Simon.

—

"I think so, Andy. She slept a lot over the last few hours, but she never really said if she was hurting. Was she unconscious?"

"I have no idea, but I would suspect so. All I could see were the trees heading for me. I just couldn't avoid them." Andy could feel himself choking up and swallowed hard. "Did I hurt her?"

"I don't think you did. Not on purpose. From what I could see of your plane, you landed it well and tried to avoid the trees. Only the slope you landed on defeated that. We'll have to make our way into town today, but I'm not sure that you're up to the walk."

"I have to be, don't I?" Andy was on his feet, hunting for his boots, returning to find Simon ready to leave.

"Okay, this is how we do it. I'll carry Oshea. You hold tight to this belt I have around my shoulder. It's about a half mile to my car, but it's down hill. We'll need to be careful."

Andy nodded, heading for the door, watching as Simon locked up and then gathered Oshea back into his arms. The men headed out, Simon watchful, Andy with his eyes on Oshea as much as he could.

Chapter 6

It had been a long hard trek down to Simon's car. Andy had stumbled many times, not quite steady on his feet, his hand tight on the leather belt. He was glad that Simon had thought of it. He would have fallen many times without it to grasp, he thought. He had been grateful for the times that Simon had paused, to let him regain his balance and his breath.

"How far to town, Simon?" Andy was in the back seat, pain evident on his face and in his movements. It did not stop him from cradling Oshea to his body, trying to protect her from the bumps and jolts.

"Not far. I only live about thirty minutes from town. That's to my cabin. Less from where I park. I'm heading for the local hospital." Simon sent a quick glance back at the young couple and shook his head. "We'll get you both looked at. But I don't think that you'll be travelling any time soon. Not for the next few days."

"I know. I'll have to find somewhere that we can stay." Andy pulled his lower lip over his teeth. "I just don't know your town."

———

"That's okay. You can stay with my sister. She takes in waifs and strays. Her husband is a good friend and is an officer. He'll be able to take your statements or hear what you have to say."

Andy nodded, weary and sore beyond what he had ever been. He barely felt the hands that helped him from Simon's car or saw them gently lift Oshea out and to a stretcher. Simon walked beside him, an eye on both before he heard his name called. He moved away from Andy and towards his friend and brother-in-law, Titus Ellis.

"Titus? You got my message."

"I did. I was planning on heading your way in about an hour but you're in town instead." Titus' keen eyes studied Simon and then looked towards the Emergency Department. "What do you have?"

"You heard that a plane went down yesterday?"

"We did. In our area. We're just starting the search."

"Head them towards Hunter's creek. The plane went down there. That young fellow? He's the pilot. The young lady? She was kidnapped two nights ago and Andy was forced to take off with Oshea and her kidnapper."

"He was? That's not good." Titus turned in a circle, feeling watched.

"No. It's not. She has no idea why. And there's a wrinkle. He works for the Barnabas Foundation." Simon rubbed at his cheek. "We'll need to reach out to them. He was about to, but then Oshea collapsed."

"He does? That certainly does put a wrinkle into it. Was she the target or him?"

"That we're not sure of. It's something that you'll be looking into. And you'll be needing to contact the police service there." Simon's steps slowed as he reached Andy's room and watched the physician and nurses work away. "We'll need to protect them somehow. I made my way to the plane and found the kidnapper was gone. Oshea seemed to think that he was dying, but he wasn't there. Who helped him?"

"That's a good question. They're not really that far from the Foundation." Titus moved to one side, his eyes on Oshea. "What happened with the lady?"

"Oshea? She seemed fine, was alert, oriented, talking. Then, she said that she was tired, put her head down, and was lost to us."

"Head injury?" Titus had seen too much on the job and this was a concern for him.

"Perhaps. Or fatigue that hit hard." Simon hesitated for a moment. "It could be either one of them, you know. I don't know that they can tell us much." He watched Andy again. "I don't think he was hurt that badly, but he was unconscious for hours."

"They'll check him out well and let us know. How be you find a cup of coffee for us both? I'll track you down once I've spoken with Amos." Titus paused for a moment, his thoughts muddled, unusual for him.

"I can do that." Simon turned and then faced Titus again. "We'll need to put us down as their next of kin. Oshea's family is pretty much non-existent. Andy has Barnabas Carey as his next of kin. I didn't get a chance to ask him about his own family."

"I'll look after that. Head off, Simon. And Lois will want all of you to come and stay with them, until they can travel." Titus shook his head. "I have no idea of what you have just become involved in, but it worries me, Simon. We'll need to pray and pray hard."

Chapter 7

Andy raised his head, rubbing at his temples. He hurt in more ways than one, he thought. *What did I go and do?* He searched the room. *A hospital room? I remember getting ready to take off on my holiday but nothing more.* He jumped as he felt a hand on his shoulder and stared at the man standing there.

"Where am I?" He had to clear his throat before he could speak, his voice rough anyways.

"You're in a hospital, Andy." Simon stared at him before he looked over at Titus. "I'm Simon. I think you've forgotten me." He pointed to the man across from him. "And this is Titus. He's the officer that I told you about. How are you feeling?"

"Sore." Andy's eyes were drawn to the room door and he frowned, causing Titus to look that way and then move out of the room, following the man who had stood there.

Simon turned to watch before he turned back to Andy.

"You'll be released this afternoon, Andy. You've been here overnight." Simon sighed, knowing

———

34

that it had fallen to him to explain what happened to the younger man. "Two days ago, you crashed your plane near my home. You were not alone. A young lady was with you as well as her kidnapper."

Andy shot to a sitting position, his eyes startled before they narrowed.

"I didn't kidnap anyone." His voice sounded loud in the room and he winced. "There is no way that I would. God wouldn't let me."

Simon's hand settled on Andy's shoulder.

"We know that, son. But she was kidnapped and then you were too."

"I was?" Andy continued to stare at the door. "But where is this?"

"This is a town not far from your home and the Barnabas Foundation. You apparently flew in circles from what Oshea said."

"I did? I wouldn't do that." Andy was becoming combative, something not usual for him. "And just where is this woman?"

"She was hurt as well, Andy." Titus had reappeared, shaking his head at Simon.

"She was? I want to see her." Andy's words died away as he slumped back on the bed, eyes closing as he slept.

"He'll keep doing that, you know." Simon gave a grin at Titus, slightly amused at the look on Titus' face.

"I know. I have spoken with Oshea. She can't tell me much more, but I will have to have her look through some of our mug shots."

"Either that or a sketch artist." Simon rubbed the fingers together on his left hand. "I spoke with an Amy at the Barnabas Foundation. She's the secretary to Barnabas Carey. Andy's parents are out west on a mission and can't be reached readily. He has no siblings. Amy said that she would have Barnabas call or come to us. He and his wife were away today."

"I see. That's that then." Titus paused, a thought running through his mind. "Was it Oshea that the man was after or Andy?"

"That I don't know. Oshea didn't seem to know much more than what she said. She's terrified, Titus."

"I know that she is." Titus' head turned as he heard footsteps and Oshea appeared beside him. "Oshea? Should you be up?"

"I have to be. Andy needs me to look after him. It's my fault that he was hurt." She reached past Titus to grasp Andy's hand, finding his tightening on hers even though he didn't rouse.

"Do we know that for sure, Oshea?" Titus' words caught at the edge of her attention.

"Of course, it's me." She looked over at Simon. "It is, isn't it, Simon? If I hadn't been on the plane, then he wouldn't have crashed."

"We don't know that, Oshea." Simon watched with compassion as she tried to process his words.

"Right now, you need to be back in your bed. Titus has someone watching out for you."

"He does? I didn't see anyone, not even a nurse." Oshea turned as Titus strode from the room in a hurried manner, not saying a word. "What's with him?"

"He had an officer on your door. There wasn't one there?" Simon's gaze went from Oshea to the door and then to Andy.

Oshea shook her head. "No, there wasn't. And I don't know why there would be."

"Because you're a victim, Oshea. A victim of crime and we need to protect you. Until we can get you and Andy somewhere safe, that's what we'll do. Put people around you like that."

"Andy needs that. I don't." Oshea turned, searching for something. Only she had no idea what it was. She muffled a scream as a woman appeared in her line of sight. "Who are you? And where did you come from?"

"That's my sister, Lois, Oshea. Remember? I think we talked about her. She's married to Titus."

"She is? I don't remember." Oshea looked up at Lois, who was somewhat taller than herself. "Can you help me? Can you help me find who it was? I don't know who it was. And I don't know what he wanted."

Lois reached to hug the younger woman, a troubled look on her face.

"I will do my best, Oshea. I'm Lois. And you're to come and stay with me. At least, that's the plan. I would like that, if you have nowhere else to go."

"No, I don't. I don't have anywhere to go. But I need to stay with Andy. I need to take care of him. No one else is." Oshea didn't see the looks on the faces of the older couple and didn't see the younger couple hesitating in the doorway.

Chapter 8

Barnabas and Aubrey Carey hesitated for a moment, his eyes on Andy before he looked up at the older couple. Simon watched him with a frown on his face.

"Can we help you?" His words were softly spoken, but startled Oshea who stared at the couple with fear on her face.

Oshea moved towards them, a puzzled look on her face.

"Do I know you? You look familiar."

Barnabas gave a gentle smile even as Aubrey's hand tightened on his.

"I'm not sure. I'm Barnabas Carey and this is my wife, Aubrey. And you would be?"

"I'm Oshea Flanagan. I'm the reason that Andy is hurt."

"You are?" Barnabas reached out a hand to steady Oshea as she swayed on her feet. "How be you have a seat? We'll talk, Oshea." He nodded as Aubrey's arm came around the other lady and she directed her to a chair. He looked up at the older couple. "Good afternoon."

"You're Barnabas. I met you years ago. I'm Simon Crocker and this is my sister, Lois Ellis. Her husband, Titus, is an officer who I think was reaching out to your police department."

"That may be." Barnabas reached to shake their hands. "I haven't been home yet. Amy tracked me down and told me where to find Andy. She didn't have a lot of detail other than he was hurt and in the hospital."

"He crashed his plane and it's all my fault." They could hear the tears in Oshea's voice. Aubrey's arm tightened around her. "It's all my fault. That man made him take us up with him. Then, he had to fly in circles. That man wouldn't let him land. Andy wanted to because there was a storm. I don't remember crashing but we did. That's when he was hurt. And it's all my fault."

Barnabas gave an inaudible sound and was in front of Oshea in a moment, crouching down to study her face.

"We don't blame you, Oshea. Not at all. Can you tell me about the man?" Barnabas' gentle words brought Oshea's gaze to him.

"I don't know. He was older, in his 50's maybe. Gray hair but he was going bald. Scruffy looking on his face. Jeans and a black sweatshirt. Running shoes. He made me go with him that night. I tried to get away but he just kept his hand on my wrist." Oshea rubbed hard at the wrist, trying to rub away the feeling of the man's hand. "I tried to get away. But I don't understand why he went to that hangar. I think he had it all planned."

"He did? Why would you say that?" Barnabas looked up, a frown flitting across his face as Titus appeared and then motioned for him to continue

Oshea shrugged. "It's just his attitude. He really didn't say much to me. And when Andy found us, he told Andy that he had to take us. He threatened to kill me." Her hand went to her side as she remembered the feel of the pistol jamming into her ribs. "I think that he would have."

"You're doing good, Oshea." Aubrey's quiet voice calmed Oshea.

Oshea stared around at the four and then was on her feet, her hand reaching to lay against Andy's face as he moved, consciousness returning to him.

"Andy?"

Andy's head turned as he leaned against Oshea's hand.

"Oshea? You're okay? You scared me."

"I did? I'm sorry. I didn't mean to." Tears briefly clouded her vision. *Enough is enough,* she thought. *I have to stop crying. I am not a crier.*

"Andy?" Barnabas moved to stand near his friend.

"Barnabas? You're here? Weren't you and Aubrey to be away this week?"

—

"We were, but you needed us. Having an adventure of your own?" Barnabas gave a grin as Andy glared at him.

Andy sighed, his eyes closing for a moment.

"I guess I am. I thought we told Dallas it stopped with him."

"Obviously not. Now, what do they say about you and where are you to go?" Barnabas raised his head to stare at Simon.

"Right here for now, I think. Simon said his sister would take us in. But I'm not sure about that."

"You're not up to travelling right now, Andy." Simon spoke up. "I've been told you need a few days before we let you do that. Barnabas, he's to be released this afternoon. Lois and Titus will take them in for now. And then we can head your way with them."

"Thank you, Simon. Lois and Titus, thank you as well. Titus? You have spoken with our force?"

"I have. To your police chief. He said he'd have a detective named Davy contact me."

"And Davy will." Barnabas grinned again. "Davy's well thought of and has worked through some adventures that our friends have had."

Aubrey shared a look with Barnabas. Both knew that Oshea's emotions were in a mix, and that how she was talking, the short sentences, the almost run together words, were not likely how she normally spoke. Barnabas had seen fourteen of his friends go through something similar as had he and Aubrey. God needed to be the centre of it all, and he wasn't sure where Oshea was on that.

Titus nodded towards the door, motioning for Barnabas to go with him. Simon followed, leaving the ladies with Andy, Aubrey standing to watch their friend. She was concerned, Barnabas could tell, but her face was neutral, not showing how much she was worried.

Chapter 9

Barnabas paced the hallway, a hand rubbing at his face, watching the doorway to Andy's room. He was at a loss, he thought. He needed his men here to help, the men employed by the Barnabas Foundation, including his lifelong friend, Breck. All the men other than Breck and Barnabas were orphans, offered employment by the Barnabas Foundation, which paid their wages and allowed their employers to hire others. Most came from different provinces and territories. But more so, he needed his father's advice.

"Titus? What can you tell me?" Barnabas finally stopped pacing, his arms folded across his chest.

"Not a lot more than what Oshea said. It's just in the preliminary stages of investigation. You will need to bring in a chopper to move his plane, I suspect."

"I'm sure of that. I'll need you to take me there so that I can assess what we need." Barnabas frowned. "I don't understand though how they managed to get to the hangar. It's enclosed with a high fence. You have to sign in and out." Barnabas' finger was in the

———

air and he had his phone out. "Breck? Hi. No, we're still away. Yes, we'll be back I suspect tomorrow. Listen, Andy's plane came down. What's that? No, he's alive, but injured. We'll need to find a contractor to come and move it for us. No, he wasn't alone. He was kidnapped, if you can believe it and forced to fly a young lady out with her kidnapper. What was that? Is he having an adventure like us? It would appear so." Barnabas gave a quick grin as he listened to Breck. "I know it was to stop with Dallas. Somehow, the memo got lost. I'm in Twinings."

"Twinings?" Breck was surprised. "That's not far from us. Did he not fly out too far?"

"It would appear not. The physician wants him to stay here for a couple of days. I'll explain it all when I see you. If you could let everyone know and get the prayer chain working, I'd appreciate that. Have you heard from Dad?"

"No, but I didn't expect to. Hold on." Breck's voice faded for a moment. "Your dad just sent a text. They're home and concerned about Andy for some reason."

"God again, Breck. I don't know how Dad does it but he always does. We'll need to find a way to contact Andy's folks. I also need you to contact the airport manager and our security people at the hangar. There is no way that Oshea and her kidnapper should have been able to be in there."

Barnabas slowly pocketed his phone, raising his eyes to meet the question on the older men's faces.

<hr>

"That was the man just under me that I was speaking with. He talked to the hangar and security there. I don't understand how they made it through our security. It's some of the best."

"Pay off? Security taken down?" Titus was running scenarios, trying to come up with what had happened.

"It might be. We have one of our men who can search it out as well." Barnabas stared once more at the door to Andy's room. "How long before he's released?"

"He'll be able to leave later today. I'll be staying with Lois. I'm a retired physician that that helps."

"God was at work, I can see. Now about Oshea? What do we know about her?"

"Not a lot, I'm afraid, Barnabas. I haven't really had a chance to speak with her. She was only on her feet once more just before you arrived."

Oshea appeared in front of Barnabas, her hands wringing against one another.

"He's hurt because of me. I need to leave." She turned, heading down the hall before the men could react.

Titus ran after her, a hand on her arm to stop her, his eyes on the man waiting near the elevator. The man stared at him and then turned and walked rapidly away. Titus frowned. Now, what was that all about, he wondered.

"Oshea, please. We need you to stay with us. You're still in danger and we can't protect you or even determine why you were kidnapped unless you do." Titus gently turned her to walk back to where she had come from.

"I know, but I'm a danger to him." She looked up, a frown covering her face as she saw Andy standing in front of her, Barnabas and Simon helping him to stand. "Andy? You're too weak to be up."

"It's okay, Oshea. We're allowed to be up. Simon is taking us to his sister's for now. Then, Barnabas will have us go back to the Foundation building."

She continued to frown at him. "That sounds ominous. What kind of building is that?"

"It's our home and office building, Oshea. We have a number of families who live there, who work for me. There is also an apartment there with your name on it." Barnabas grinned at her.

Aubrey gave her husband's arm a swat even as she smiled at Oshea, an arm coming around her as she turned her to walk towards the elevators, Lois on her other side.

"We have a building that has a number of apartments in it. The men who work for the Foundation live there with their families. They also have offices on the main floor. And we have a number of apartments or suites if you like that are offered to people in need."

"Oh, that wouldn't be me. I don't fit that." Oshea yawned, suddenly overcome with fatigue. "I need to sleep."

—

Barnabas swung up into his arms as she suddenly slumped, a brow quirked at Simon, who laughed.

"She did that yesterday. Just dropped off to sleep. This way. Let's get them to Lois and Titus' and then we can sort it out as best we can."

Chapter 10

Two days later, Andy stood in front of Oshea, a puzzled look on his face. She was adamant that she couldn't be around him. Only she couldn't tell him why. He thought that they had moved past that but obviously, he thought, they hadn't.

"Oshea, please? Just listen." Andy reached for her hands, finding hers icy cold. She's so afraid, dear Lord, and I just want to relieve that, to make it all better for her. "I know Lois has said that we can stay here but I need to go home. Or at least back to the Foundation building. I would like you to come too. We're not losing contact with Simon or Lois or Titus. They won't let us."

"I know what you're saying, Andy. But there are little ones in the building, you said. I can't bring danger to them." She drew her brows down in a glare as he began to laugh.

An arm around her, he guided her to the love seat in the living room and made her sit, his arm still around her.

"It's not funny, Andy." Oshea tried to rise, only to have Andy's arm tighten more around her. Simon watched with amusement from the doorway, wondering who would win.

"It's okay, Oshea. Each of the men and their ladies had what we call an adventure. Some almost died. In fact, one of my friends was drowned and brought back to life."

"That doesn't happen in real life." Her eyes were huge as she stared at him, leaving Andy to feel as if he were drowning in them. The thought passed through his mind that he didn't want to be anywhere other than where she was.

"Well, it did. It even happened to a police detective friend of ours." Andy bit at his lips, his heart praying for his lady as he already thought of her. "Simon, has Titus been around?"

"Not today. He had to be away. That's why I'm here and Lois isn't. They're away for a few days." Simon approached to sit in a chair near them, his eyes thoughtful.

"I see. We've taken you from your life then, have we?" Andy stared down at Oshea. "I think I need to go home." His words paused as the doorbell rang.

Simon was on his feet, greeting Barnabas and then looking at the man, slightly older than Barnabas, who stood beside him.

"Simon, good to see you. This is Davy, a detective on our force. He's here to talk to those two."

"Those two? Oshea who wants to run away? Or Andy who wants to run home?" Simon grinned at the two men.

"That the situation, is it?" Davy moved past him, pausing to study the young couple, a frown momentarily crossing his face. He knew Oshea. Knew that someone was looking for her but not for her good. Now, he had to figure out how to keep her alive and healthy and to keep Andy from getting hurt once more.

Andy looked up, a grin on his face.

"Davy? You're here?"

"I am. How are you, Andy? And didn't you know the adventures were to stop?" Davy grinned at Andy as he began to laugh, startling Oshea.

"I know they were but it seems as if the good Lord had other ideas. I shudder to think of what might have happened to Oshea otherwise."

Oshea stared at Davy, not quite certain of who he was and what he wanted. Davy simply stared back at her, accepting the cup of coffee that he was handed with a quiet word of thanks.

"Oshea Flanagan. I seem to remember meeting you at some point."

"You do? I'm sorry. I don't seem to remember you. I guess that I should." She puzzled through the people who she knew, not recognizing him at first.

"Not necessarily. You were a witness to an accident that happened about seven years ago. I was one of the responding officers. You were in our town."

"I was? I'm sorry. I don't seem to remember." Her voice died away as memories tumbled through her mind. Horror covered her face. "He was there. He was in one of the cars."

"Who was, Oshea?" Andy's head tilted so that he could see her face. He was shocked at the look on it, the abject horror.

"My kidnapper. Davy, can you find him from then?"

Davy's notepad and pen were out as he made notes.

"We will certainly try. Now, about what happened. Talk to me, Oshea. I know that you've been given a statement. But I need to pick your brains and see what else you can remember. It doesn't matter how trivial or unimportant. Sometimes those are the memories or things that can trigger a resolution to your adventure.

Chapter 11

Davy finally tucked away his pad of paper and pen, his eyes thoughtful as they rested on Oshea and then Andy. Oshea really hadn't given him much more information than he had. He shook his head at Andy, knowing that he would have to question her again and again, until she could remember. There was something there, he knew, that she was tucking away, not forgotten really. It was what happened, he knew. People wanted to forget the danger and all that trauma when they were scared. And right now? Davy knew that Oshea was terrified. He just didn't know why or by whom.

Andy rose to walk to the door, eyeing the sky. It was getting dark, he thought.

"Will she remember, do you think, Davy?" Andy's hands jammed down into his jeans' pockets.

"She will. They usually do. It may take another event to have it happen. I pray that it doesn't. Just prepared for that." Davy hesitated to say more, knowing that Andy was well aware of what to expect. They had talked not that long ago on what the others had faced.

"It's not something that you can really prepare for, though, is it?" Andy turned his head to stare back at the door, his thoughts on Oshea. "How do we do this, Davy? How do we protect her and yet move forward?"

"That's not something that I can really tell you." Davy stared down at the wooden steps that he was standing near. "Each one has to decide on their own how to proceed. Oshea will do that, just as you will. Stay close to her, Andy. I know that's what you want. She'll fight you on that, I can see that."

"She will. She already is worried about the kids at the Foundation Building. I talked to her about going there."

"I thought that you had. Just remember. You can't force her to go where you want her to. She has to make that decision." Davy glanced at Andy, seeing the struggle going on with his friend. "Stay close to her, pray for her, be her friend. Don't smother her. That's always a danger with us fellows. We want to keep our ladies safe and we have to let them have the freedom to make their own decisions."

"I know. It's hard, you know." Andy swayed for a moment, Davy's hand coming out to steady him. "And I have to do something about my plane."

"You do. I have been given a copy of the report as I am sure you have been. It will be a while working through the system, as you know."

"I know. I just wish I knew what he wanted. It was just so strange." Andy turned slightly as he heard a sound from behind him. "Oshea? What is it?"

———

54

"I don't know, Andy." She moved towards him, tucking herself close to him. "Davy? How do we find out what he wanted?"

"That's what we work on, Oshea. We talk to the police in your town, here, and then we look into what is going on with Andy. It's not an easy process or a short one. There is danger around you. We can't have you running around on your own."

"I know." Oshea's head went against Andy's shoulder without her realizing that she was trusting in him that much.

"You can't stay with Lois and Titus forever, you know. That's why Andy has suggested that you move back to our town, to the Foundation building. We do have security there, even though it has been breached at times. We won't let you lose contact with Simon, Lois, and Titus."

"I know. I just don't know what to do." Oshea's voice died away. She was lost in thought, Andy and Davy could see.

Davy finally excused himself and drove away. His thoughts remained on the two that he had left behind him. He was definitely going to need to speak with Will Peters, police chief in their town, and maybe talk to Dallas Chisholm, a retired detective, who might have some ideas for him. He knew Andy and the men of the Foundation, having been an investigator on most of their cases, as well as working for the Foundation at present.

Andy simply stood and held his lady, not acknowledging to himself that was how he thought of

—

her. He stiffened his knees to keep himself upright before Oshea stirred, her eyes on his face before she turned them to walk back inside the house. Barnabas watched them, before he smiled to himself, thinking that Andy had found his lady and found her when she was in danger. Just like all the other fellows, he thought, and just like himself and Aubrey.

"Andy? If you want to head back to town today, we can." Barnabas shared a look with Simon. "Simon, you're welcome to come with us."

"You know, I would like that. I have wanted to see your building for a while now. I saw it when it was being built but haven't made it back there since. Oshea? Andy? Up for a road trip?" He grinned at Oshea as she stared at him.

Chapter 12

Her mouth open in surprise, Oshea stared at the Foundation building, not expecting anything like what she was seeing. Barnabas and Andy shared a grin, Simon just watching quietly. Her mouth snapped shut and she turned to Andy.

"I didn't know it was like this!"

"It is. It's home to the families of the Foundation, Oshea. And you are welcome. Barnabas will set you up in a small suite on one of the floors. I'll be here for now." Andy paused. "I need to reach out to Mom and Dad."

"We've done that for you, Andy." Barnabas pulled into his parking spot and turned off his vehicle. "Someone was heading their way to see how far along they were in their task and if they were at a point that they could leave it."

"I'm sure they are. Dad would have made sure to have the bulk of the building done by now." Andy bit at his lip. "I just don't know that they'll leave though."

"They will, Andy. You know that. You're too important for them not to." Barnabas dropped down to the ground, watching as Andy carefully slid out, a grimace and groan coming from him and smiled as Oshea was beside Andy, a hand tucked around his arm.

"Andy? You're hurting. What are we to do?"

"Come along, Oshea. We'll show you where you two will be. Doc and Anna are around somewhere, Andy. He'll be wanting to assess you."

Andy gave a nod, too sore to do anything other than that.

"I know. And he'll need to look Oshea over as well." He saw her puzzled look. "We have a physician and his wife living here. Doc and Anna. He works as an Emergency Room physician and she's a retired nurse." Andy looked up as he stepped into the foyer, watching Oshea's look of awe.

"This is huge!" Oshea's eyes travelled around the foyer, seeing the seating areas on either side, each with its own fireplace, the hardwood floor, the security desk near a corridor, and then her eyes moved up. "That is beautiful. I love those stained glass windows."

"Mom was the one behind that." Barnabas smiled as she stared at him. "Mom and Dad are away right now but they'll be around."

"Barnabas? How can you do this?" Oshea was puzzled. "I don't understand how you can afford a building like this. And Andy says that you pay the men's wages?"

"We do. It's part and parcel of being encouragers, just like Barnabas in the Bible." Barnabas went to continue when Oshea spoke.

"You're named for him. And that's what the Foundation does, is it?"

"You understand correctly." Barnabas' gaze went to Simon who nodded.

"I see." Oshea stared at the apartment door that they had stopped in front of. "This is mine?" The men could see tears in her eyes. "I can't afford this. I have nothing with me."

"That's okay, Oshea." Andy's hand on her back directed her through the door. "One of the wives will have been around with clothes for you. Her parents run the homeless shelter and she is always collecting clothes for there. She donates to whoever has a need, and that would be you at the moment. And if I know another lady's twin sisters, they will have gone shopping for you."

"They would? Without knowing me? That's cool." Oshea moved away, walking through the apartment, finding as Andy had said, clothes piled on the bed for her and other items in the ensuite bathroom.

"Andy? We've set you up right next door." Barnabas handed him a set of keys. "Simon, we have an apartment for you as well. Andy, come find me later."

Andy nodded, watching as Barnabas closed the door behind him.

"Simon?"

"I know, Andy. You need to sit. Let me see what they have in the kitchen for a meal."

Andy nodded, sinking down gratefully at the kitchen table.

"They'll have shopped for us. There's likely coffee in the cupboard." His head turned as he felt Oshea near him and simply reached for her hand. "Okay, sweetheart?"

Oshea shrugged, her mind puzzling out why he referred to her as sweetheart.

"I think so. They've done too much." She stood again, reaching to help Simon find food and beverages for them. "Do they have tea?"

"More than likely. Andy said someone shopped for you." Simon turned her back to sit, placing plates of sandwiches down and then reaching for mugs, pouring coffee for Andy and himself and tea for Oshea.

Chapter 13

The next morning, Oshea was up and out of the building, finding the walkways and then the gardens. It was early enough that the sun had just cleared the horizon. She didn't see the security guard following her. She stopped, her face turning up to the sky, her eyes closing as she drew in a deep breath. *This is nice,* she thought. *I could handle living here, but I need to go home. Only I don't want to. It's not home any more,* she thought, and could not understand her feelings, not knowing that Andy had claimed her heart when she wasn't looking.

Andy paused as he found her. He had been concerned when she didn't answer her door and he had begun a search. Titus had called, as early as it was, warning Andy that the man had been seen in Twinings and was likely heading his way.

"Andy?" Oshea stopped in front of him, fear on her face. "I don't like the look on your face."

"It's okay, sweetheart. I just wanted to find you, to share the morning with you." He reached for her hand, turning her to walk towards the rose garden,

—

61

waiting until she had seated herself on a wrought iron bench before he sat as well. "This is nice."

"It is. Someone went to a lot of work, didn't they?" She reached for a yellow rose, bringing it up to her nose to inhale the delicate scent.

"They have. They did this as this is home to the men. Now that there are children here, they are working to make it more friendly for the youngsters."

"I see." Oshea grew quiet. "Andy, is it over?"

"What over? This adventure that we seem to be on? No, it's not. I need to talk with you and I just don't want to spoil the morning."

"You must. Who called you?" She watched him closely.

"Titus did. Your kidnapper is alive and well and was seen in Twinings. Titus said that he's heading this way."

"I would think he would. How do we stop him? I don't understand why he took me in the first place." Oshea frowned, trying to sort through her thoughts and finding it difficult with Andy sitting beside her, her hand still tucked in his.

"I don't either. I know the men here will work on your mystery as they can."

"They will what?" Oshea was not certain that she had understood him correctly.

"The men work away on finding the bad guys, as the twins call them, and finding the evidence that is needed. They each work in a different occupation and that helps in how they find the information. They all think differently. Dallas will be involved, I know, if he isn't already. And Davy is like a terrier with his cases. He doesn't let go until he solves it."

"But how can they do that? I won't have them taking time from their work or their families." Oshea was upset, her body beginning to shake with her emotions.

"They won't let that happen. If needed, Barnabas and Breck pull them back in to work on it. Their employers are in agreement with this."

"That's a strange way to do things." Oshea grew quiet, her eyes on Aubrey as she approached and then sat down across from them. "Aubrey? You're here?"

"I am." Aubrey smiled. "I have come to find you. I know Doc wants some time with Andy and you will be at loose ends. I want to spend time praying with you and then finding out about your life and what you do for work and where you want to be."

"That's a tall order." Oshea shook her head. "Some of that I not likely can answer."

"Didn't think you could. It's a process called life that we're living." Aubrey rose, reaching for Oshea's hand and drawing her to her feet before she linked her arm with hers. "Andy, you're on your own. Doc's in the infirmary."

"I'll head that way. Then, I have the insurance investigator to meet at the airport." He sighed. "And I'll need to find a driver."

—

63

"Taken care of. Brady's around and volunteered. That way, he says he can keep an eye on you." Brady was a paramedic and a close friend. Aubrey grinned at him as he shook his head.

"Come and find us when you're done. We'll be around somewhere." Aubrey watched as Andy headed for the building before she turned to Oshea. "Now, Oshea? What would you like to do? You're free here to make your decisions. The fellows don't step in unless they have to. And I know that Andy will back you in whatever you decide, unless it's a matter of life and death. All the guys do."

"He will? He shouldn't." Oshea watched as Aubrey led her to one of the sitting areas. "These are nice."

"They are. Now that we're all married, these have become the gathering spot for us. There's a chapel as well as an infirmary."

"Someone planned well. I don't know that I have seen a building such as this." She looked startled as someone laughed and then sat beside her. "I'm sorry. I've brought trouble here."

Hagen laughed more heartily at that. "You have no idea what we've been through. I'm Hagen, by the way. My sisters helped to shop for you. As to danger, let's just say that our friend, Bradon, was drowned and revived and his wife, Ennis, was stabbed. If Doc or Brady had removed the knife, she would have died."

Oshea's eyes were huge by the time that Hagen had finished speaking.

"That's not going to happen to me, is it? A plane crash was bad enough."

"That is one thing none of us has experienced." Fynn spoke up as she sat beside Oshea. "I'm Fynn and I was stabbed and left in the dirt with a box ready to stab me with something to kill me. I was left for my creepy crawlies to find."

Oshea stared at her in turn.

"Creepy crawlies?" She stumbled over her words. "I'm afraid I don't understand."

"I'm an entomologist. Brady, my fellow, loves to tease me about them."

"This is quite the building, isn't it?" Oshea stared around. "How many are there of you?"

"Fourteen." Hagen laughed at the look on Oshea's face. "That's right, fourteen with Barnabas. Breck is right under him and looks after the guys. Then each of the guys works outside the building and volunteers as well."

Oshea shook her head, unable to comprehend fully what she was being told.

"You're overwhelmed." Aubrey took pity on her. "We'll continue to explain it to you. but for now, we just want to spend time with you and pray for you. And then, we'll start working on your adventure. I know the fellows already have."

"They have? They can't." Oshea was almost in tears at the thought.

Aubrey reached to hug her.

"We've all been where you are, Oshea. So we can understand to a certain extent how you are feeling."

Chapter 14

Andy turned from the hangar, a frown on his face. He didn't understand how Oshea and her kidnapper had made it through security.

"Did we find out how they got in, Dan?" He spoke with the airport manager.

"There was a blip on the feed early that morning. That's likely when they came in. Davy's been around and said that an abandoned car was found just outside of the fencing." Dan paced to the open door of the hangar. "I just don't understand why you."

"That's what has me puzzled. You know me, Dan. I don't have anything in my background that would lead to this." Andy stood beside him, searching for what he just didn't know.

"I know. What about the lady? What's her background?"

"Oshea? I'm not sure. We really haven't had much of a chance to talk. I know Davy was heading back to speak with her at some point." Andy rubbed at his forehead, a headache growing.

Brady was watching him closely and approached.

"Are you about done, Andy?"

Andy shook his head, regretting it.

"No, the insurance investigator is heading this way. In fact, that is likely him." Andy frowned. "No, that's not him." He paled. "The kidnapper. How did he get in?"

Brady was moving Andy away, heading for an office, Dan standing in the way. The door locked behind them, Brady forced Andy to sit, pulling out his phone.

"Davy? Andy and I are at the airport. The kidnapper just showed up. How did he get in?" Brady could hear Davy's running footsteps.

"I'm on my way. A patrol vehicle was almost there, Will had asked for that." Davy's voice faded for a moment. "Are you two safe?"

"We are. I've managed to lock us into an office. But Dan was there." Brady worried about Dan, knowing that he could well be hurt.

"Did the man see you?" Davy's voice was loud for a moment and Brady winced.

"I have no idea. Andy saw him and then I moved him to the office." Brady waited, his eyes on Andy. "Andy, how bad is the headache?"

Andy looked up through blurry eyes.

"It's bad, Brady. I don't know if I've ever had one this bad. I need to get over them. How can I ever fly again if I don't? And flying is who I am."

"I know, Andy." Brady searched, finding some over-the-counter pain medication. "Here, take these. It will help. And you will fly again. God isn't done with that part of your life just yet."

Andy nodded, regretting that, before his head was down on the arms that he had folded on the desk. Brady's eyes shifted between Andy and the door, before his phone rang.

"Brady? Davy. We're here. Dan's okay. And we have the kidnapper. Dan was able to keep him here. Stay put for a few moments until I come find you." Davy paused. "Andy?"

"He's fighting a bad headache, Davy. I need to get him home where he can stretch out."

"I know. It won't be long."

Andy barely raised his head as he listened to Brady. The headache was beginning to ease but the heartache for his lady was only beginning. He wanted to be with her but he wasn't sure if he should, not knowing which one of them had been the target.

"Brady? How do we know which one of us it is?" Andy's gaze found Brady.

"Which one of you? That's what we're working on. We know you, Andy. Know your family. That we can research without too much difficulty. It's Oshea. We need to talk with her and find out that information from her. Find out what she did and who she knew. Who her parents were."

"I know. Simon may help. He's been able to talk with her, he said. And then's there Titus and Lois. Lois had long conversations with Oshea. This is tough." His eyes closed for a moment as he contemplated what he was going through and just life in general.

"We know, Andy. We know. You know what we all went through. You were involved with the search for Cadee's parents."

"I know. That was difficult. And Jaxcy's parents. The ladies will need to tell their stories to Oshea. She really doesn't believe me, you know." Andy gave a smile as he remembered how adamant she was that it didn't happen and that it wouldn't happen to her. She didn't have a fellow. *Not yet,* Andy thought, *but I would like to be that one, Oshea, the one that walks beside you for the rest of our lives.*

"You said Aubrey had found her? Fynn had talked to Aubrey early and was going to find them. They'll help her, Andy, just like each one helped the other." Brady rubbed at his face. This is getting old, he thought. *Lord, how many more of my friends are going to go through this, face life-threatening and potentially life-altering events. I know that You are in control but it is just too difficult for us.*

A tap at the door interrupted their talk. Brady listened and then unlocked the door, allowing Davy to enter. He saw the officer that took a position just outside the door.

"Davy?" Brady was puzzled, his eyes on Andy, who had sat up to watch Davy as well.

"Andy? You're okay?" When Andy simply nodded, Davy shook his head. "He was that close to you, Andy. If Brady hadn't moved you away and kept you out of sight, you would have disappeared. They would have used you to find Oshea. What is her story? What do they want that badly?" Davy was angry, not at Andy or Oshea, but at the situation. It took a lot to anger him but this had.

"I have no idea, Davy, but we need to find out. Can we leave?" Andy was on his feet, heading for the door, stopping only when Davy's hand found his arm.

"You can, in just a little while. Right now, we're clearing out the hangar. Something has to be here for them to know where to find you. Your phone?"

"It's at the Building. I forgot it this morning." Andy's eyes closed for a moment. "And you will need to look it over, won't you?" His words bit at Davy who shared a look with Brady. "When does this stop, Davy?"

Chapter 15

Looking up as she heard footsteps, Oshea's smile lit up her face. Andy reached to hug her before he sat beside her, Fynn moving so that he could. Fynn's eyes were on Brady, seeing the shuttered look in his, and sighed. What happened, she wondered? Something had for Brady to look like that.

"Having a good time, sweetheart?" Andy grinned at the ladies who had surrounded Oshea. Almost all of them were there, just Imly and Neasa missing.

"I have been. They've been telling me their stories." Oshea snuggled closer to Andy without realizing that she had, feeling safe for the first time that day with him near her.

"They have, have they?" Andy studied her face. "We need to talk, sweetheart. Davy's here."

"He is?" Oshea's head turned as she heard the worry and something else running through Andy's voice. "What happened?"

"Your kidnapper, Oshea. That's what happened." Davy's voice was grim. "Somehow or other, he managed to get to the hangar again. If Brady hadn't moved Andy to an office, Andy would have disappeared. It would not have mattered to the man if he had had to harm Dan or Brady. So, tell me, Oshea, what does he want?"

"I have no idea. I'm not involved in any crime. I haven't seen or heard anything that I shouldn't have." Oshea stared at him, her brow wrinkling as she thought through her life. "I don't know why. You can look at my family and talk to them. Not that they'll be really concerned about me. They have made that obvious."

"We will do just that, Oshea. I just need to know if you have any idea or thoughts about why." Davy was grasping at straws. If he didn't find something soon that he could investigate, the case would need to be set aside and would grow cold. He didn't want that for his friend.

Oshea shook her head once more.

"I'm sorry. I really don't know. I can give you a list of names, relatives, friends, work contacts that I know for us all. Would that help?"

"It would, immensely. Thank you for offering, Oshea." Davy was on his feet, walking away, leaving Oshea staring after him.

"Did he really just do that?"

Andy grinned as his arm tightened around her.

"He did. If he has any other questions, he'll be back. And he will. You'll need to get used to him being around."

"That's what I'm afraid of." Oshea sat, her thoughts muddled, not sure what she was needing to do. Her gaze fell on Simon and she rose and walked over to him. "Simon? Did I say anything to you that might help?"

Simon shook his head, his eyes on her face, knowing what she was asking.

"Not really, Oshea. We mostly talked about what had happened. You may have said something to Lois and perhaps that Davy needs to speak with her."

"Okay. I can put her name down. And Titus." She blew out a breath. "This is hard, you know."

"I know it is. You have a wonderful group of men and ladies here who will help. Davy's good from what I am told. And Titus will continue to work his end. Until he can solve why you were kidnapped, he can't really close the case on the plane crash."

"No, he can't, can he? How do we do this?" Oshea turned to study the lobby, seeing for the first time the men who had joined their ladies. "There is a seriously large group of people here."

Andy laughed as he joined her, searching the group and seeing them all there, including Dallas and Deri.

"There are. And I understand that tonight is a potluck supper. They do this every few weeks."

"A potluck? I have nothing prepared." Oshea worried at her lip, trying to think what she could prepare on short notice.

"It's okay, Oshea. You can bring something for another meal. Tonight? We are just happy to have you and Andy with us. That's what our family does, Oshea. They open up to welcome others into it." Neasa, Breck's wife, stood in front of Oshea, Breck beside her.

"That's exactly what we do, Oshea. Andy?" Breck moved Andy away, intent on speaking with him only to find Oshea with them, refusing to let go of Andy's hand. "Oshea?"

"He's hurt because of me. I have to make sure that he's okay." Tears momentarily blinded her. "I don't cry, you know."

Chapter 16

Two days later, Oshea stood at the window in the living room of her suite. She stared out at the rain as it teemed down, the weather matching her mood. She had not heard from Andy at all that day and it was now noon. She worried about him and then sighed. Oshea turned, her eyes studying the suite, liking what she saw but knowing that she had to leave it. Only she wasn't certain that she could. She wasn't prepared to leave Andy behind and leaving meant that.

A tap at her door had her cautiously approaching it, to stand peering through the peephole. She frowned. She didn't know the man who stood there. Her phone ringing had her almost running to where she had left it in the bedroom.

"Oshea? It's Neasa."

"Neasa? Where are you?"

"Right outside your door. Barnabas' dad is with me. Can you let us in?" Oshea could hear the smile in Neasa's voice.

"I can. I saw him but didn't know him." She opened the door to find Neasa, Aubrey, and the older gentleman smiling at her.

"You did well, Oshea, not to open the door. I'm Bruce Carey. Can we come in?" He pointed behind her.

"Oh, of course. I'm sorry." Oshea moved back, watching the trio closely. "You're here and you must have a reason for that."

"We do." Neasa held up a box. "I have our lunch. I was in town early and picked up some salads and fruit. I hope that was okay."

"It is, but you didn't have to." Oshea was not used to how the ladies treated one another. It was nothing like what she was used to in her own life.

"I know, but we did. Now, let's eat. Bruce will want to pray with us, and then he wants to talk with you, Oshea."

"That doesn't sound good. I don't know anything, that much I can tell you." Her disgruntled voice had Bruce laughing.

"You might without knowing it. But I don't want to talk about your adventure. I want to talk about you, find out what you do for a living, and if you want to work here in our town."

Oshea was quiet during the meal, leaving the others to talk among themselves, drawing her into their conversation as she would let them. Aubrey and Neasa cleared the table, watching Oshea as they did so, before they seated themselves again, their eyes on Bruce.

"Oshea, you don't know me. The first thing I would like to do is to pray for you and Andy and this situation that you have found yourself in. It's not of your making, I wouldn't think."

"It's not. I just don't understand. Davy said that they arrested the kidnapper and that he was facing charges in other places." Oshea drew a deep breath. "If that's the case, I think that I can leave and go home."

"We don't want you to. Not yet, Oshea. Not until we know for certain that no one else is after you. Let me pray with you." Bruce was as soon as his word, his head bowing as he prayed for Oshea and for Andy.

Oshea decided as she listened to him that she had never heard a prayer such as his. She felt that God was right there in the room with her. She blinked when he finished, coming back to reality, as she watched him.

Bruce studied before he reached for a folder. The information that he had found, or rather that the men had found and handed him, concerned him. He wasn't quite sure how to approach Oshea, not knowing how she would react to what he had to say.

"Mr. Carey, what is that you want to talk to me about?" Oshea's words were hesitant.

"First, call me Bruce. That's what everyone does. Now, what do I want to talk to you about?" Bruce tapped his folder. "In here, young lady, is a proposal for you. Let me tell you about the Foundation. I inherited a lot of money and invested it and started the Barnabas Foundation. It is worth billions, but God is the one that we serve. The money is used for Him and in His service. I am on the board of the Foundation but Barnabas is the one who runs it. Breck serves under him as the overseer, for want of a word, for the men. Neasa does that for the ladies. If you have any concerns or anything at all, find Neasa or Aubrey.”

“Now about you? What did you do for work?”

“Me? I worked in a convenience store. I know that it wasn’t a career, but I enjoyed it. I just didn’t know what I wanted to do. Mom and Dad weren’t happy with me but then they weren’t happy with much I wanted to do.”

“What are your dreams, Oshea? What was one thing that you really wanted to do but couldn’t?” Bruce watched with compassion as she struggled to understand what he was really asking her.

“My dreams? I am not sure that I have ever had any. I know I did want to go to college but that was out of the question. I had the marks to get in but I just didn’t have the funds and loans were always turned down.” She refused to look up, jumping as Aubrey’s hand landed on hers and squeezed.

“What would you have studied, if you could have?”

Oshea shrugged. “I’m not sure.” She looked up at Bruce, finding him watching her intently. “I always loved languages but that is something I had never thought of studying. I was going to try to get into an optician program, but that just didn’t work out. I’m sorry. I’m really not sure what I would have done.”

———

"I see." Bruce looked down for a moment before he nodded. The board had met that morning, their weekly meeting. Barnabas had raised the situation with Andy and Oshea. The board members had looked at one another and then nodded. "The Foundation board met this morning. For the last month or so, we have been praying about a situation where we were looking to find the right person to work in it. It involves the elderly and handicapped in our church family. Many are trying to stay in their homes but are having difficulties with managing their homes, their finances, and just life in general. We have been impressed as a whole that we needed to find the right person. When Barnaba spoke to us this morning, just to update us on what is going on with you and Andy, we all felt the Lord directing that position to you."

Oshea stared at him, dumbfounded at his words. Bruce smiled gently at her, knowing she was confused.

"You are not to give me an answer today. Pray about it. Talk to any of the ladies, to Anna, to my wife, Elizabeth. To Lois from Twinings. Talk it over with Andy. We don't want you to rush into this. We are fine with however long it takes for you to make your decision."

"But I'm so dangerous, Bruce. What if I bring harm to one of them?" Oshea was worried, but her heart had begun to beat faster, having found someone who saw something in her, without knowing her and offered her hope.

"We understand that, Oshea. If you undertake this before your adventure is over and the ones responsible arrested, I have spoken to our security team head. There would be a security guard with you at all times."

"There would? You would do that for me, a stranger?"

"Not a stranger, Oshea. Never a stranger. Just a sister in Christ that we have just met and want to get to know and fellowship with. That's what these ladies are here for. They will pray with you and answer any questions that you may have. I will be available at any time that you need to talk with me. Take your time to pray it over. This is something that we do, Oshea. We pray about a position that we want to develop. When we are confident of that position, then we pray for the person who will be chosen by God to fill it. When we have confirmation of who to approach, then I approach that person on behalf of the board and offer it to them. We give no timeline for an answer. That person is instructed to pray about it, waiting for God's leading. If they say that God has closed the door to it for them, we pray about the next person. This is His work, not ours. These are His funds, not mine. Not the board's."

"A good person to speak with would be Locklin and Buckley." Neasa spoke up. "Buckley was the minister of our church until they were offered their position in the Foundation. They prayed about it and felt that God wanted them to move on. He is missed sorely as our pastor but he is where God wants him. They will both counsel you."

"They would? Then I guess I need to speak with them." Oshea sat, lost in thought, not hearing the ladies cleaning up after their meal and the three leaving quietly.

Chapter 17

Andy approached Oshea the next morning, finding her sitting in one of the areas in the lobby. He had just spoken with Titus, who was frustrated at the pace of the investigation, did Andy know that? Andy had laughed, said he was the same, and just what did Titus want. Nothing, Titus had informed him, other than to make sure Andy and Oshea were well.

He sat, his arm coming around her, finding her leaning against him without a word. He prayed for her, sending that she was unsettled.

"Sweetheart? What's wrong?"

Oshea sighed. Of course, Andy would have found her. That's what he did, didn't he?

"Bruce talked to me yesterday. They want me to take on work with the Foundation."

"Only, you're not sure if you should. You're praying about it?"

Oshea nodded and then leaned harder against him.

———

"He told me to talk to you. I should but I just don't know what to think."

"What was it they offered you?"

"A position working with the elderly and handicapped in the church, helping them to stay at home."

"I see. And you're not sure about that?"

Oshea shook her head.

"I'm not. Bruce said that they would have a security guard with me if necessary but I don't know what to do."

"Knowing Bruce and the board, they have not set a deadline on your response. Pray about it. We can discuss it as much and as often as you want." He stretched out his legs, content. The headache was lessened today but still there enough that he could feel it. "And how are you feeling, other than that?"

She shrugged, her eyes on the door. She wanted to run, to the threat away from him, but she knew that if she did, he would only follow her.

"I don't know. Do you know where everything is at in the investigation? I called Davy but he was in court."

"No, I'm sorry. I have no idea. Davy will call us back, that much I know. Now, what can we do with you today?"

She looked up at him, thinking how tall he was and so good looking. A sound at the door had her feet, her arms wrapped around herself. Andy was on his feet as well, an arm around her.

"Oshea? What is the meaning of this? What are you doing here? And why aren't you at work?" The man who stood in front of her was angry.

"Dad? How did you find me?"

"It wasn't hard. A detective called and then I traced it back to here. I should have known that a man would be involved." Her father reached for her arm, pulling her towards him despite protest.

Andy stepped in front of her, causing her father to withdraw his hand and stand in a threatening manner. Andy simply tucked Oshea behind him and stared at the man.

"She's here of her own free will. She is also under police protection from our force. She won't be leaving." Her father tried to reach around Andy to grab at her arm but Andy simply moved back into his way. "Oshea, run for the security desk. Now." He heard her footsteps scurrying away even as he watched her father.

"That won't stop me." Her father headed after her, to come to an abrupt halt as a number of men appeared in his way, including Davy. "Out of my way. I have come for my daughter."

"And she's not leaving with you." Davy walked towards her father, forcing him backwards. "This is a private building. Right now, you are very close to being arrested for trespassing."

"Trespassing? I don't think so. I am taking my daughter and leaving." His fist came back and then slammed into Davy's chin, sending the detective to the floor. Her father's arms were caught and pulled behind him, Brandon and Brady doing the deed.

"That was a mistake, my friend." Andy reached to help Davy to his feet, a hand on his arm to help steady him. "If I'm not mistaken, you've just been arrested for assaulting a police officer."

"What officer? No one identified themselves as such." Her father was belligerent even when Davy pulled out his identification. "That doesn't mean anything."

"On the contrary, it does. I've been wanting to have a conversation with you. That happens now, at our police detachment. There are officers here who will escort you to town. You're in pretty serious trouble."

Oshea's father was led away, still protesting. Davy rubbed at his jaw, grateful that it was just bruised.

Oshea was beside Andy, her hand on Davy's arm, staring at the door her father had just disappeared through.

"I'm sorry, Davy. I had no idea he would do that." They could hear the horror in her voice at what her father had just done.

"Not your fault, Oshea. You don't need to apologize." Davy squinted at her against the pain that he was feeling. This had not been one of his better days, that much he knew.

"I still have to." Oshea stood, her eyes on the door. "I still don't get how he tracked me to here. No one would have told him."

"Maybe not. But if they knew that it was Andy who you were with, all they had to do was ask about Andy. Knowing that he was employed by the Foundation, it wouldn't take a lot of thought to connect you to here." Barnabas stood beside them. "Davy, you are here for a reason?"

"I was but I'll have to come back." He pointed at Oshea. "No running away. I don't want to have to track you down." He walked away as she protested that.

Chapter 18

Standing behind the window to an interrogation room, Davy listened to the venom spewing from Oshea's father. He had not expected to hear what the man was saying. He shook his head. What was it with the Foundation building ladies? In trouble and the guys just had to come to their rescue. Only, technically, Andy was not one of the building's inhabitants. He had his own home in town. And he would soon head back there, Davy knew, albeit reluctantly.

Will stood beside him, a frown momentarily on his face.

"Are you okay, Davy?"

"I am, Will. I just never saw it coming. I don't think any of us did. Oshea was in total shock." Davy puzzled it over. "He shouldn't have known where she was. I thought we made that clear to Titus."

"I spoke with him. He has no idea how her father found out where she is. He hadn't told anyone other than Simon and Lois. And neither one of them would

---

87

have said anything. I spoke with Simon yesterday as he was heading home. He's worried about her."

"We all are." Davy's attention went back to Oscar Flanagan. "He's not giving up, is he?"

"Not at all. He's also not asked for a lawyer. We're not speaking with him other than to lay out the charges. He'll be here for a while. What about her mother and brother?"

"She hasn't said much." Davy frowned, pulling his mouth into a tight line. "From what little she did say, they're not close."

"I see." Will hesitated and then walked away. The investigation was in good hands, he thought. Only it weren't going anywhere.

Davy watched him walk away and then turned back to the window. He frowned once more before he was away, heading for his office. He searched his paperwork, finding the notation that he had made and then nodded. He needed to speak with Oshea before he headed for her town just a little ways away from them.

Andy watched Oshea carefully, not certain as to how to approach her. Her father showing up like that? It had shocked him to say the least. And he knew that it had frightened his lady. Now, he needed to deal with that for both of them.

"How did he find her?" Branigan spoke from beside him, trying to puzzle through what had happened.

"I don't know. Titus was adamant that he hadn't said anything. And we weren't in her town." Andy sighed, knowing that the investigation had just expanded.

"So, is he tracking her somehow?" Branigan looked around. "You said she doesn't have her phone. Is she wearing any jewelry?"

"A ring and her watch." Andy's eyes flew to Branigan before he was walking rapidly across the lobby to where Oshea saw with some of the ladies. He could see the security guards moving around outside the building. He crouched beside her, his hands reaching for hers. "Oshea? Your jewelry? Can we see it for a moment?"

Oshea stared at him before she gave a small nod and pulled the ring from her finger and then undid her watch band to hand him the watch. She had no idea why he wanted them but she gladly gave them to him. She had liked neither the ring or the watch but felt compelled to wear them as they were gifts from her parents.

"Did you buy these?" Branigan took them from Andy, his eyes on Oshea.

"No. Mom and Dad gave them to me. Just in the last year. They've never done that in the past. So why did they?"

Branigan examined the ring and then the watch, a small tool in his hand to pry off the back of the watch. He sighed. It was as he had expected.

"They're tracking you, Oshea. There's a small device in the watch that does it. Did you ever replace the battery?" His keen eyes studied her reaction.

Oshea shrugged. "Dad did. About three months ago. I didn't think it needed to be done but he insisted." She rose, to stand beside Branigan. "What is that?"

"A tracking device, Oshea. Do you have any idea why?" Branigan watched with compassion as her face crumpled and then as Andy simply swept her into his arm.

"Why?" She broke from Andy, running for the stairs.

The group in the lobby watched as she disappeared from sight. Andy stood, anger on his face before he spun and headed for the door, stopping as he remembered that he had no vehicle and couldn't drive yet anyway.

"Andy?" Breck stood beside him. "Where would you like to go?"

Andy shrugged, working at tamping down his anger.

"I don't get it, Breck. Why?"

"That we'll work on. God is in control, Andy. We both know that." Breck stared out at the horizon, not sure how to proceed with his words.

"I know, Breck. I just wish it was different." Andy studied the ground in front of him, not willing to admit how much Oshea had come to mean to him.

"She's your heart, Andy. We can all see that." Breck's hand rested on Andy's shoulder. "We've been there, Andy. You've walked it with us, although not as closely as you are now."

"No. I thought we told Dallas it ended with him." Andy's grin briefly creased his face.

Breck began to laugh. "That we did. Don't let Buckley around you. He'll suggest a date for a wedding for you."

Andy turned to Breck in shock, seeing Buckley standing beside Breck for the first time, a wide grin on his face.

"And that I would, Andy, but you two are nowhere near that yet. At least, I don't think you are." Buckley was known for having offered dates for weddings to some of the couples. He was teased about that by the couples, knowing that they had no hard feelings towards him.

"No, we're not. I'm not sure that we will ever be." Andy's face grew thoughtful and then sad.

"She's interested, Andy." Barnabas spoke from beside him, the men of the building gathering around him. "She's just not certain of you and likely thinks it's too soon."

Chapter 19

Oshea paced her apartment three days later. She was feeling caged and wanted her freedom back. Only she wasn't sure how to go about that. Sighing, Oshea reached for her keys, heading for the lobby and then the outdoors. She stared around, her focus on a building not too far from where she stood. Heading that way, she paused as she heard her name called.

Hagen headed her way, her young son and daughter in tow. Heath ran ahead towards Oshea, his little arms coming up for her to pick him up. Not to be outdone, his twin sister, Hannah, struggled to get down from her mother's arm with the same intent towards Oshea.

"Oshea! Just who I wanted to see. No, Heath, you don't need up." Hagen grinned at Oshea as she bent to pick up the little fellow. "No, Hannah. You're not going to Oshea. You two are getting too big to both be held at once."

"They are so adorable." Oshea hugged Heath and then reached out a hand to grasp the little one Hannah was waving at her.

—

"They are and they are a handful at times." Hagen pointed to the building. "You were heading that way."

"I was. I was feeling caged. And that something big was about to happen and I don't want it to." She flushed. "I'm sorry. I shouldn't have said that."

"No, it's okay. We've been there. This building is the gym. The board keeps it updated for us all. There's a walking track as well. And in the back of the building? That's my shop."

"Your shop?" Oshea followed. "I don't understand."

"I do wood puzzles and educational toys. It's my business. It was a dream that Dad and I shared. It has grown and I have been able to hire staff. Come on in and I'll give you a tour. Today? The staff have the day off. I do that every three weeks - give them a day off just because."

"That's so thoughtful." Oshea wandered the shop, her interest taken with the different toys and puzzles. "You have been a lot of work into this."

"I have. God has blessed me. At one time, I didn't think that I could even continue. Brandon helped me get through that." Hagen paused, her eyes on Oshea. "Oshea, you're troubled."

"I am. I can't figure out why the tracking device. Did they not trust me that much? I know that they were taken up with themselves and what they were doing. But still, they're my parents. Aren't they supposed to protect me?"

—

"In a perfect world, yes. But we live in a broken sinful world. Parents don't always take care of us, protect us. In fact, they can be our enemies and wish us nothing but harm. That happened with Ker, with Neasa and her step parents. God walks with us, Oshea, every step of the way. He knows what we will face and provides the strength for us to get through it. He also provides those whom we need in our lives at the time. For me and the girls? It was Brandon. Even though he did forget us for a time, he still tried his best to protect us."

Oshea had turned to watch Hagen, her arms holding Hannah who had cuddled down against her. Heath had stopped at their toy box and was going through it, determined to find the one toy that he wanted.

"I guess that I never thought of it that way. So, you're saying that God provided Andy for me? To help me walk through this? I can't let him. He's already been hurt because of me. And had his plane destroyed." Oshea grew sad at that thought.

"He's not looking at it that way. He's thankful that he was there. It could have turned out so much worse, you know. But none of us can understand how you managed to get to the hangar, not with the security that's there."

"I think the man bought off someone. Somehow, the gate was unlocked and we walked in. He left his car on the road. He didn't seem to care if there were cameras." Oshea paused, a sudden light on her face. "He walked right in, right in plain sight. Wasn't there anyone else there that day?"

"There was. Mechanics. Security people. The airport manager. How did they not see him?" Her phone was out and she sent off a quick text to Branigan. "Branigan will look into that. The guys are meeting in the conference room with Andy, brainstorming as to what happened. Then, they'll begin their research."

"Conference room? Research? I don't understand." Oshea turned as Hagen's sisters entered.

"Holly. Haley. Take the twins. I'm taking Oshea to the conference room. Lock up for me." Hagen grasped Oshea's hand and pulled with her, back to the building and then down a corridor to the conference room. "In here. They've set it up like a detective office, as Darby says. That's Berneen's brother, in case you didn't meet him. He was in on the shopping that the girls did for you."

Oshea stopped just inside the door, her jaw dropping as she saw the activity. The men were there, deep into their research, comments and teasing flying back and forth. Her gaze moved to the walls and she saw the white boards, already with information on it. Andy turned from where a kitchenette had been set up and then headed her way, his head tilted as he watched her.

"Oshea?" His quiet voice beside her had her jumping as he startled her.

"Andy? What is all this? Hagen said they were working on this, but I don't understand."

"This is how they are the hands and feet for God as we go through this. They've done this for everyone, including Dallas and Deri. That's Dallas at the board right now. He was a police detective until he took on a position here at the Foundation."

"I see. And what do they plan on finding out?" Oshea was tired, tired of feeling that her life was spiralling out of control on her.

"They plan on finding out why and who." Brady had approached, assessing her as he did so. "They will work on it as they can, not taking time from their own duties or their families. If it comes to the point where we need to, then we pull back from our work and concentrate on this. We will solve it for you, Oshea and Andy. Make no doubt about that."

Chapter 20

Simon turned as he heard footsteps on his deck, extending a mug of coffee to Titus. He sighed. He had spoken with Andy and was dismayed to hear that Oshea's father had found and tried to remove her from the Foundation building. He knew that he had not given out any information, but somehow she had been found.

"Titus? How did he find her?"

"That we don't know. I spoke with Barnabas. He said something about a tracking device in her watch."

"A tracking device? Her father?" Simon rubbed at his neck.

"That's the supposition, given how he's reacting. And he's up on charges of assaulting a police officer."

"That's what Andy said. What do we do to help them?" Simon had come to care deeply for the young couple.

"That I'm not sure of. Barnabas said the men were working away on it as was the detective, Davy. But they don't have a lot of information."

"I don't get it, Titus. Why here? It's as if this was the destination." Simon turned to watch Titus.

Titus nodded slowly before he sipped at his coffee. That had been his thought, and he had spoken to Davy about that. Neither one of them could see the connection to Twinings for either of the couple.

"Davy had the same thought. Only, we don't see why." Titus sighed. "This has just gotten bigger and bigger.   And Davy said that he has to set the investigation aside for now. Unless new information comes up, he has nothing to work with. The kidnapper isn't talking, not even to the lawyer the judge assigned to him."

"He's afraid?"

"That's the supposition. Or he's playing games with us."

"Did you ever get a name on him?"

Titus shook his head, frustration evident in his movements.

"No. He's not in the system that we can see."

"That's not good. I'm thinking of heading that way tomorrow, just to see how they are."

"Lois will want to go with you, that I know. She was asking if I had spoken to them."

"I'll stop and get her then." Simon's thoughts drifted off, back to his conversations with Oshea.

—

"She's afraid of something, Titus. Only I don't think that she realizes she is. She would be hesitant about wording and people when we talked. I just can't put my finger on who or why."

"That's what we're all getting. Andy will work with her on that. And I am sure the ladies will." Titus grinned suddenly. "Did you hear their stories?"

"The gist of each one. It is amazing that they all went through something but survived. And for some of them to marry as they did?"

"I know, but from what I hear, God chose each one for the other. The Foundation is blessed to have that family of believers. They reach out so much to their community."

"That they do." Simon set his mug down. "Now that you're here, I have something for you. I've written down as much as I can remember of my conversations with the two. Maybe you'll see something in that. I need to get copies to Oshea and Andy and also that Davy."

Titus nodded, his thoughts on someone else. "There is one person that I need to reach out to. Maybe she can find something that we've missed. She's good that way."

"Sure. Whatever it takes to solve this for that young couple. I like them. I hate to think of them going through what the others did."

—

Chapter 21

Andy walked away from his medical appointment three days later. Frustrated that he was not yet cleared to fly, he was at loose ends. Brady had offered him a ride into town that morning seeing as Andy was not yet cleared to drive, and he had promised to come back. Only Andy was done early with his appointment. He stood for a moment, staring down at the river from the bridge that he stood on, watching as the water flowed beneath it. *Lord, You had me come aside for a time. I don't know the reason for that. But my heart is heavy. I want to fly for You but can't. Are You telling me something? Telling me to find something else to do? Flying is who I am. It's a part of me that I don't know if I can ever give up.*

Not noticing the men who had stopped behind him, Andy moved to walk away. He stopped short as he felt hands on his arms and then something digging into his back. He simply nodded as he was forced to move away, no pedestrians around to see him taken captive once more.

Shoved into a vehicle, Andy studied the men, trying to remember as much of them as he could. But

———

then the blindfold dropped over his eyes prevented that. His hands were bound. Andy feared for his life, not knowing what was happening.

Dragged from the car, his feet tangled with each other for a moment before he found his footing. A hand on his arm forced him to move forward, towards a building that he could not see. In a room by himself, he heard the door close but not lock. His hands had been freed and the blindfold removed. He was puzzled. The men had not said anything, not even to threaten him.

Turning an hour later as he heard the door open, Andy watched as the man approached. Government, he thought. The man was short and dressed in a suit, a folder in his hand.

"Andy, I'm sorry that we had to bring you here this way. We need to speak with you."

"Yeah, well. You could have just asked. I would likely have come. And just what government department do you work for?" Andy waited for the man to speak and then headed for the door. "I'm out of here."

"Andy, one moment, please. I will leave this with you and we will take you home again. Your lady is in danger."

"My lady? And just how do you know that?" Andy spun to stare at him.

"This." The folder was up in the air as the man spoke. "We have word that her parents are involved deeply in illegal activities. We need your assistance to protect her while we're working to find all the information and proof that we need to arrest them."

Andy reached for the folder and then walked through the door. He didn't see anyone around him. Stepping outside, he was surprised. He was still in town, near where he had been taken. His walk took him back to the medical building, finding Brady watching for him.

"Andy? Where were you?" Brady frowned at him.

"I was done early and went for a walk. Let's get out of here. I need to talk with all of you."

Andy's hands rested on the file folder, not seeing the looks that Brady was shooting at him. He was puzzled. Just who were those men? And why him? He was a pilot, not an investigator.

"Brady, are the men all around?" Andy's quiet question finally broke the silence in the truck as Brady parked at the building.

"Some are. What's with the folder?"

Andy shook his head, his eyes dropping to it.

"I need to talk to you all or as many as are around. Something happened and it involves Oshea and the government."

Brady shot him another look and then sighed. This has just gotten deeper for him, Brady thought, and Andy really doesn't know what to do.

"And I need Oshea in on the conversation. Was she with the ladies this morning?" Andy paused inside the door. "And I really want to go home."

"We know you do, Andy. This isn't your home. Nor is it Oshea." Brady headed for the conference room, hearing Andy's steps behind him. "And Oshea? I think Fynn was heading her way this morning. She's quite taken with your lady."

"My lady? No, I don't think so, Brady. Not likely to happen." Andy stepped through the conference room doorway, searching for who, he wasn't quite sure. He felt someone moving into his space and felt the hug. Looking down, he was surprised to find it was Oshea.

"You're back, Andy. I was so worried about you." Her voice was muffled against him.

"I'm here." He nodded his thanks as Brady took the folder from him. His arms wrapped around her. "Are you okay?"

"I am now." She looked up at him, thinking again how tall he was. And good looking. "I felt something had happened to you."

"There was. And I need to speak with you about it." Andy turned her back to the room. "You've been here for a while?"

"Not really. Fynn and Berneen were around and talked with me. And then Cadee and Anna showed up and we prayed. These ladies are so precious. They have been through so much but their faith is so strong." She blinked rapidly. "I need that."

"It's coming, sweetheart. I can see it already."
Andy led her to a table and made her sit, sitting beside
her. "I had a situation come up when I was in town
that I need to talk to you about. It involves your
parents."

Chapter 22

Oshea stared at the hand Andy had planted on the folder. She frowned. He was worried and upset, that much she knew but not why.

"Andy? What happened today? How did your appointment go?"

"It was okay, a disappointment if you must know. I'm not cleared for flying, not yet. He didn't know when yet. I have to wait a couple of more weeks at least, he said." Andy bit at his lip, not sure how to continue. He could hear the silence in the room and knew without looking that all eyes were on him. Andy looked up, finding Buckley watching him.

Buckley nodded, before he began to pray. Andy and Oshea needed that, he knew from experience.

"Okay, Andy." Breck spoke up even as he looked around. All the men were there as were their ladies. Doc had slipped in, sitting quietly down near Andy where he could monitor him. "What happened?"

Andy held up the folder. "This. I went for a walk to the river while I was waiting for Brady. I know. I shouldn't have but I needed to think. While there, some men approached me, made me go with them, blindfolded and bound. I was shoved into a room, my bonds and blindfold removed. A while later, a man entered. Suit, tie, shiny shoes. Shouting government department of some sort. He simply stated that they needed my help in an investigation. Handed me that folder and then just let me walk away. It was the Douglas building, Breck. You'll want to look into who has that. Anyway, they said it was to do with Oshea's parents. They were involved in something, only they didn't say what. He said it was in the folder."

"And you haven't looked yet?" Breck nodded as Andy shook his head. "Then, we look at it together. Oshea? Did you have any idea?"

Oshea blinked as she thought through what Andy had said.

"No, I wasn't. Dad has his own business. I never really understood what it was, though. He travelled a lot, overseas including. Mom works with him. My brother? He works there too. I'm not sure doing what. I guess I just wasn't interested enough in his business to ask what it was all about. Maybe I should have."

"It is likely just as well that you haven't." Branigan spoke up. "We've been looking into it, Oshea. We're finding that your father's business has been under investigation for trading secrets with foreign governments."

"Trading secrets?" Oshea paled. "And someone thinks that I know what they are? Is that what this is about?"

"We don't know for sure. We're still in the preliminary stages of that investigation." Brennen spoke up. "But we have had word that someone else is after you. That we don't know why."

"You mean, more than one? One wasn't enough?" Oshea rose and began to pace, Andy's eyes on her. "But where does Andy come in?"

"That we don't know." Brandon stared at Andy. "Andy, I think it's because you're a pilot. We have traced some of Oshea's father's flights. They coincide with some of yours when you've flown overseas with some of the board or Bruce or Barnabas."

"They do? And somehow, someone thinks that I have knowledge of what he was up to." Andy's eyes slid closed as his head dropped back. "But I have never met him. You can't say that I met with during that confrontation in the lobby."

"No, but we all know how these guys think." Brendon took up the tale. "Just being in the same country and yes the same city would make you suspect. They likely have been following you for a while."

"I think you're right, you know." Andy stared down at Oshea who had returned to sit beside him. "For the last few months, I have felt followed. Just a sense of someone watching me. Nothing that I could go to the police with. They can't investigate suppositions and feelings.'

"No, they can't, but we can now." Davy had appeared to stand beside Andy. "Were some of these times overseas?"

Andy slowly nodded, his mind working before he reached for a pad of paper and a pen, writing quickly and tearing off the sheets to hand to Davy.

"These places." His hand rested back on the folder. "And then there's this."

Davy sat, his hand reaching for it.

"May I, Andy?"

"Sure. I'm not really ready to find out what is in it, but I guess that I, no we, have no choice."

Chapter 23

Davy slowly opened the folder, not quite sure what it would contain. He stared down at the one sheet in it, a frown on his face as he read the information. No, he thought, this is not right. Something is off about all this, including how Andy had been taken and then just let walk away. Governments just don't do that.

"Andy, can you describe the man for me?" Davy kept his voice low.

"I think so. Forties, short, heavy set to a degree, shaved head. Blue eyes. He was dressed in an expensive suit and silk tie, I think it was." Andy paused, not quite sure what was wrong. "It just seemed off, Davy. He showed me no identification and he should have. Just the way it was all done seemed more like it was the mob or criminal than on the up and up."

"That's what I thought." Davy's finger tapped the page. "I recognize the names here. They are not government. I would say that you walked away with God's help, Andy. Now, we need to keep you and Oshea safe. And just how do we do that?"

Andy shrugged. "I'm released to drive, so I'll be heading home." He heard a faint sound from Oshea and looked down at her. "I can't stay here, Oshea."

"But what will I do? I can't stay here without you." His tightened on hers, keeping her in her seat. "Andy?"

"You can stay here." Andy was suddenly on his feet, pulling Oshea with him, drawing eyes to them as he hurriedly walked from the room. He moved to the sitting area in the lobby, looking around before he was out of the front doors, heading for the rose gardens. Oshea sat, watching as Andy paced before he was on the bench beside her, reaching for her hands.

"Oshea, I know that you are scared. I am too. I don't want harm to come to you. Only I don't know how to do this."

"To do what? Protect me? Protect you? I don't know either, Andy. I am just so scared for you." Oshea didn't continue, but she could have. Her feelings were in her eyes and on her face and Andy could only stare at her.

"Oshea? Tell me? Do you care for me? I find that I love you."

She nodded. "I think I do. Andy, what are we to do? I can't go home, not knowing if Mom and Dad are involved in something. After the way Dad acted? I don't want to be around him. It just wasn't right."

"No, it wasn't." Andy swept her into a hug, praying as he did so. He looked up as Buckley and

Locklin appeared and sat on a bench facing them. "Buckley?"

"Andy? Oshea? We don't want to intrude, but may we pray with you two? God spoke in an urgent manner for us to come and find you." Buckley was as good as his word, praying for them both.

Oshea sat back against Andy, his arms around her, feeling safe for the first time in months, she thought. That disturbed her and she didn't know why.

"Andy?" Buckley's unspoken question broke into Andy's thoughts.

"Buckley. I know why you're here. And Locklin. We need help, Buckley." He stared down at Oshea. "I think that we would like to marry, for now. Oshea needs someone and she's not comfortable staying here, even though she should be safe."

"I see." Buckley's eyes turned to Oshea. He had spoken with her but not at great length. He knew that Locklin had but she had kept Oshea's confidence, not saying what they had spoken about. "Oshea? What are your feelings?"

"My feelings?" Oshea blinked in surprise. "You know, I don't know that anyone has ever asked me that. Not in my entire life. I am scared, petrified would be the word I would use. You know what happened with my father. My mother and brother have not reached out to me and they should. That leaves me on my own. What do I do? I know what Andy is asking even though he hasn't said the words. It would be unfair to put him at risk."

———

"He's already at risk, Oshea. The plane crash proved it. So did today. Whoever it is? They are determined that you and Andy are somehow mixed up in this together." Buckley shared a look with Andy. "Okay, so we think about it. Andy?"

"I know, Buckley. We haven't known each other for long. But look at Baird and Berneen. Or Brennen and Jaxcy. They didn't know each other before they were forced to marry. And look how much in love they are. God worked in their lives."

"And He can and will in ours. Andy, Oshea. I am not getting the sense from God that He has said no. On the contrary, I am sensing that He has put the two of you together. Does this mean marriage? Not necessarily. But it could. Andy, when do you move home?"

"Today is Thursday. By Saturday, I would like to. But that depends on Oshea."

"I see. Oshea? Other than what you have said, do you have any objections?"

Oshea turned her face up to Andy, studying the man. She shook her head.

"I have none. But we need to pray about this, I think."

"You do." Buckley sighed, a wry grin on his face. "At least you have time, I think."

"Not as much as we would want, Buckley." Andy felt a sense of urgency. "We need to do this, if we are, now."

"Okay, then. Locklin, if you'll go with Oshea. Oshea, your identification. We'll need to head to town, Andy."

The men were away before Oshea could say anything. Her face crumpled for a moment as her emotions got the best of her. Locklin hugged her, a prayer whispered in her ears.

"Come on, Oshea. We have some planning to do. As for a wedding dress, I am sure one of ours would fit you. We will gladly share with you."

"You would? I'm not used to this."

"It's what we do, Oshea. Share. Now, let's find the ladies. Buckley will have stopped and told the men, if I know him. He'll perform the ceremony for you, unless you want the regular minister."

"Oh, I don't know him. I know Buckley, at least sort of." Oshea stared at Locklin as she went off in gales of laughter until she thought through what she said. She began to giggle. "I didn't phrase that very well, now did I?"

Chapter 24

Andy watched as Oshea moved among his friends and their ladies and families. It had been a gruelling, emotion-filled few hours, working feverishly to arrange the wedding, and then standing waiting for Oshea to appear in the chapel. Doc had stepped in to escort her to him. Oshea had approached him, dressed in a beautiful gown. Which lady had offered it, he wasn't sure, but he would find out and thank her.

Buckley stood beside him, watchful and concerned.

"You have doubts, Andy."

Andy sighed.

"I do, Buckley. She was rushed into this and it's not fair to her."

"She agreed to it, Andy, knowing that it was rushed. She has a peace about her that I don't see often."

"She does. I guess that I do as well. It's just now how I expected this to happen. I wanted Mom and Dad here."

"And they are, Andy. They arrived just before the ceremony. They had to leave for a bit to speak with Davy but here they are." Buckley moved aside as Andy's parents approached him.

His father, Stephen, studied his son before he hugged him, holding him for a longer time than normal. Their relationship had changed that quickly. His mother, Sarah, reached for him next. Andy took comfort in the mother hug.

"Andy? Are you sure?" His father's hand rested on his shoulder.

"I am, Dad. Not how I expected it, but she's in danger."

"We know, son. We have spoken with Davy. Now, where is your bride?" Stephen looked around, finding Oshea hesitating to approach them. "And this is Oshea?"

"It is, Dad." Andy wrapped her to him, his hug welcoming to Oshea. "Oshea, these are my parents, Stephen and Sarah."

Stephen studied his new daughter and then just swept her into an unexpected hug. Her parents didn't hug, Oshea remembered, and she just couldn't understand why. Sarah was waiting, her mother hug as welcome as Stephen's father hug had been.

"Oshea, a beautiful name for a beautiful lady. I am so going to enjoy having a daughter. We wanted one but God told us that we only had a son." Sarah smiled at her son. "You are welcome to our family. Now, what do we do?"

Oshea stared at her and then began to laugh, tears near the surface.

"I have no idea. Andy?" Oshea looked up at him.

"The ladies have prepared a meal for us, I think. We just mix and mingle and enjoy ourselves."

Later that evening, Oshea paced her suite. Andy had escorted her there and she knew that he had slipped away to the suite he had been using. She sighed. *Lord, I have no idea what we're doing. You seem to be leading us. It would be nice if You would let us know what to expect.* She had changed from her dress into what she called her grubby clothes of leggings and a long T-shirt, something that she would never have worn at home. She hadn't been able to eat much of the meal that had been served and decided that she needed something.

Heading for the kitchen, Oshea paused in the hallway, watching as Andy moved around that room. He turned as he heard her, an uncertain look on his face.

"Oshea, we need to talk. I have never taken you to my home."

"No, you haven't. I don't know where it is, what it's like, what you expect from me." She waited, not approaching him, not sure on where she should be.

"I know, sweetheart. We will. We'll do that over the next few days. Right now, you're hungry. You didn't eat a lot tonight. Here, sit." Andy waited for her to do just that and then served her, despite her protest.

Early the next morning, Andy sat up on the couch from where he had slept. He looked towards the hallway and sighed. *This is going so well, Lord. You are here in the midst of all this, but I can't see that right now. Today, we'll move to my place and I need Oshea to feel comfortable enough to make it hers. Right now, I'm not confident that she will ever do that.*

Oshea stood where she couldn't be seen. She had not slept, spending the time in prayer instead. She had a peace about what they had done. She just wasn't sure how it would affect their lives or how safe either one of them would be. And that scared her. No, she thought, terrified her.

Chapter 25

Davy shoved open the door to the conference room, raising the heads of the six men who were there, working away. He needed to pick their brains, find out what they had discovered, and then contact that Emma at Trackers. She would help, he knew, and right now, he was at a loss. Oshea's father was refusing to talk as was the kidnapper. He had gotten nowhere in his search for the men who had taken Andy two days ago.

"Davy?" Baird looked up once more as Davy paused beside him. "You're here? Good news or bad news?"

Davy sighed as he slumped into a chair.

"How about no news? What have you fellows dug up?"

Baird pointed to a stack of files.

"That. We have printed off what we have found, confirmed it all, and have it ready for you. Benen took photos of the boards for you. Emma has been in touch. She said that she's sending you what she has and she doesn't like what she's finding."

"She's not? I'm glad she's on board. What have you found out?"

"That Oshea's parents are deep into something, and that involves foreign governments. He has contracts for IT work with some departments and we have evidence that he's been tracking them."

"This has just snowballed, hasn't it? And whoever he's working for wants to put more pressure on him using Oshea? What about her brother?"

"So far, he seems to be in the clear. He's not working the IT portion of the company, rather the financial. But there seems to be a problem with the financial portion as well."

"Of course, there would be. And is he the problem there?"

"No, not that we can find out. In fact, I just found out that he has left the company and moved from her home town. I'm tracking where he's gotten to." Bradon spoke from beside Davy, even as he dropped another folder in front of the detective.

"He has? That sudden? And why?"

"I'm still working on that." Bradon shrugged. "I've left a voice mail for him to call me, that I wanted to speak with him about Oshea. I'm not sure if he will call me back or not. You have his number?"

"I should do. Let me speak with him about this. You're just touching base about Oshea?" Davy's keen eyes watched Bradon.

"I am. It's not right how she's been cut off from her family. I am trying to find out if he was part of it or not. She seemed to think that he was."

"Okay. Keep it to that. If he says anything else, have him call me." Davy was on his feet, stopping to speak with each other the men before he gathered up the folders and disappeared.

Baird stared after him before he looked around.

"That was odd, guys."

"I know. Davy's on the trail of something. Only he's not sure what or if he's even right. But his street instincts are leading him that way." Bradon spoke for the group. Davy had been an undercover cop for years before he left that and moved to the detective squad.

"We'll need to speak with Oshea soon about what we've found." Brendon sighed. "And I can guess that it will likely be me that does that."

"You and Breck, I think." Barnabas has appeared, listening to their conversation. "Andy said that they're trying to settle in, but Oshea is still unsettled."

"She will be, until we figure out why." Bradon was on his feet. "I'm off, fellows. I'm due for my volunteer work." He walked away, leaving the rest looking at one another before they looked at what they were doing, set it aside and each walked away, ready to return on another day to pick it up.

Chapter 26

Roaming through Andy's sprawling bungalow, Oshea felt at peace but also unsettled. She snorted to herself. That was a mixed up way of looking at things, she thought, but that was exactly how she felt. She liked his home, her home now, she thought. She sighed to herself. What would her parents say? Oshea had no idea if her father was still in jail or not. She had refused to ask Davy when he stopped by earlier that day. He had looked at her with a somewhat amused gleam in his eyes but he didn't volunteer anything.

She turned as she heard Andy's footsteps, watching him closely. He was still hurting, she thought, the headache still not gone. Please relieve them, she prayed. He needs to go back to his choice of careers and can't.

"Did you get settled in, sweetheart?"

"I did, Andy." Oshea bit at her lip. "I'll need to go and pack up my apartment. Not that I have a lot. It was a furnished one that I found about a year ago."

"We can do that. Brody asked me about that earlier today. Some of the men will go with us. They won't let us go on our own. And knowing Breck, he'll have some of the security team go with us."

"He will? Okay, that's good, I guess." Oshea stood for a moment, uncertainty in her stance.

"We'll get there, sweetheart. One day at a time." He swept her into a hug. "Davy didn't say much today."

"No. I asked him, and he shook his head. He's having to set it aside, isn't he??"

"For now, but he won't forget us, if that's what you're worried about. The fellows are working it as they can. And Emma, our friend who finds people others can't, is working it. She said she should have something in the next day or so."

"Andy? What are you to do? When can you go back to flying?" Oshea was worried about him.

"Soon, I pray, sweetheart. But for now, I'm working through some plans with Barnabas. We're looking at bringing in another pilot and letting me do some training. I have my instructor's license but have never really used it."

"You can teach? Can you teach me? That has been one thing that I always wanted to learn. How to fly. Only I couldn't say anything. Mom and Dad would have been vocal about that."

"They were like that? You won't find me like that. I'll back you in what you want to do. All I ask is that we discuss whatever it is, weigh the pros and cons, and make a decision together. If you make a decision about something on your own that you feel strongly about, I back you unless it means you are in danger. Then, I step in." Andy watched her face, seeing her acceptance of his words. "Now, what do we do with the day?"

"I think that I would just like to stay here, study your home and yard, see what you have done. Your mom called."

"Did she?" Andy waited, knowing that Oshea was still uncertain about her welcome.

"She asked if we could come for a meal but that she understood if we said no. I said I'd talk to you."

"If you wish, we can go. Or we can stay home. I won't force you to go, sweetheart. That's a decision we make together."

"We'll go then. I like your parents. They are so different from mine." Oshea hugged him and then moved away, walking back through the house that was now her home. "Andy? Are we to expect bugs, threats, letters, packages, whatever it is that usually comes?"

Andy trailed after her, his thoughts puzzled for a moment.

"More than likely. I know Davy had someone go through the house and search outside for us today. He'll do that for now."

"He will? And if we find something, does he take care of it?" Oshea stared at Andy's office, not seeing it. "Did he ever say how the kidnapper got into the airport property?"

"Not yet he has. That's something that's part of the investigation. He may not say anything until it is finished."

"I see. It was just so strange how he walked us in." Oshea's brow lowered. "How did he know that you were there? I can remember him muttering your name."

"You never mentioned that before."

"I didn't? I thought I had. He knew who you were and who you worked for. I had the impression that he had researched you and then staked out the airport. You know, the gate was open when we went through. I was facing away from it. He had made me do that. Then, just after I heard a vehicle, he pulled me through the gate." Oshea paled. "He planned this."

"I had thought that. We'll need to let Davy know this." Andy sent off a quick text. "Now, I wonder if that's how he did it the second time as well."

"It might be. Andy, what did we get mixed up in?" Oshea was suddenly more terrified than she had been.

Chapter 27

Davy stared at his text message. How did they come to that conclusion, he wondered? He looked around and then down at his desk. He had too many investigations on the go, and right now he had to set Andy's off to the side. He would not forget it, that he promised himself. Will had spoken with him at length about his cases, just as he did with all his officers. He was concerned that they didn't burn out.

Walking to the front of the building, he stared at the man standing there. Burnie was there, beckoning to him.

"Burnie? What the secret?"

"I need to talk to you about Oshea. I don't think that she's a natural daughter to her parents."

Davy nodded as he thought through Burnie's words.

"That's not the novelist in you coming out is it?" Davy grinned at Burnie as he shook his head. Burnie was an author of suspense novels.

"No, it's not, although it would make a good plot in one of my novels. No. It's just that I've seen their pictures. They don't look like one another. Her brother? She doesn't look like him but he looks like their parents."

"Are you saying we have another Neasa?" Davy rubbed at the back of his neck, dismayed at the thought.

"I wonder if we do. I have asked Emma to look at that and she has promised to do so. Only she's been called in on an urgent investigation and can't right at the moment." Burnie was worried about his friend. "We need to figure this out before Andy or Oshea get hurt again. Simon called me, asking what he could do."

"I'm sure that he is concerned but I can't see what he can do. Other than pray. And I know he's doing that, as we all are." Davy thought through what he could say and sighed to himself. There wasn't a lot that he could. "Andy said that they've settled back into his home but that Oshea wants to head to her apartment and close it up."

"That's what we wondered. We're planning on going with her and there will be security with her. Sending some officers?" Burnie smirked at Davy as he laughed.

"No, it sounds as if you have it under control. But I will speak with an officer there when she goes. Just let me know the date." Davy walked away, leaving Burnie at loose ends.

Burnie turned for a moment and then headed for the library. He had some research to do for a book and needed to get at it. But Andy's adventure kept interfering in that. He had an idea that he wanted to run with and that meant research, something that he loved to do.

Raising his head hours later, Burnie blinked, staring at Davy sitting quietly across the library table from him, his eyes intent on Burnie.

"How did you know, Burnie?" Davy went right to the point.

"Know what?" Burnie was confused for a moment, his thoughts still deep in the research he had been immersed in for his next novel.

"Oshea? Her brother? They're biological siblings. Her parents? Friends that were to look after them if something happened to their parents. Only, we can't confirm that anything did. They were not originally from this area." Davy watched as Burnie thought what he had said over.

"Then, this makes sense." Burnie hunted through the pile of notes that he had made and found the one sheet that he was looking for. "I found this, but wasn't sure what it meant. It gives names and dates."

Davy reached for it, his eyes not dropping from Burnie for a moment, seeing the agitation in his friend. Dropping his eyes to read what Burnie had discovered, Davy was dismayed. Burnie had found information before they had.

"How did you find this, Burnie?"

Burnie shrugged. "I have no idea. I just treated it as I would a plot line and went from there. And Jace from Emma's office has confirmed it. I forwarded you his email."

Davy nodded once more, not having had a chance to retrieve or read his emails. It had been that busy of a day.

"I see. I'll look at that and then I'll have to go and talk with Oshea." He was on his feet, moving away, leaving Burnie staring after him before Burnie shook his head, gathered up his research, and left, not seeing the man watching and then following him.

Chapter 28

Moving away from the door so that Davy could enter, Andy studied his friend. There was something up, he knew, something that disturbed Davy greatly. He prayed suddenly for his bride, fear rising within him. Oshea stood in the kitchen, a letter in her hand, a letter from her mother that terrified her.

"Davy? I thought you wouldn't be around for a while." Oshea went right to the point, handing him the letter. "And you need this."

"I do? What is it?" Davy glanced at the letter and then focused on Oshea.

"That letter is from my mother. Only it scares me." Oshea backed up into Andy's arms. "It's not like her at all. What changed?"

"Can we sit?" Davy sat, watching as Oshea hesitated before she pulled out a chair to drop into. "What scares you about it?"

"It's not like her. The wording. The threats. I didn't do anything to warrant that." Oshea pointed at the letter. "So why?"

———

129

"I'll come to that. First, how are you feeling?"

"Scared. Terrified. Worried." She glanced at Andy, finding him nodding. "I want this over, Davy, and now. Andy needs to heal and he can't, not properly."

"We know, Oshea. We are working on it." Davy hesitated, not sure how to proceed. "Your brother?"

"Odell? What about him?"

"He's missing, Oshea. I wanted to speak with him. He's not at his apartment and hasn't been. I asked the police force there to do a welfare check when I couldn't raise him on his phone, given the situation with you. They found evidence that he had been forcibly removed from there."

"Odell?" Her hands covered her mouth in shock. "Why? He didn't do anything, did he?"

"Other than leave your father's employment, put in his notice at his apartment, and tell friends that he was leaving town. That if you weren't coming back, he wasn't staying there."

"He did? I never expected that. I mean, we had talked years ago about what we would do as adults, but I thought that he had forgotten that. He seemed distant as we became adults." Oshea was not certain now that she had been reading her brother correctly.

"He has. We're actively looking for him. This has just changed the severity of what you are facing. He may well have been taken to make you cooperate with them."

"I wish I knew who they were. I'd confront them." Her hands tightened on one another.

"Not a good idea, Oshea." Davy signed as he felt his phone vibrate and pulled it out, reading the text message before he shot a look at Oshea, Andy watching closely.

"Davy?" Andy's brought Davy's attention to him. "What news do you have?"

"Not about you or Odell. Oshea, please, if you know anything, talk to me." Davy hesitated to ask the questions that he knew he must. "Did you or your brother at any time suspect that you were not the biological children of your parents?"

Oshea frowned at him, pondering his question. She shrugged. That had never crossed her mind.

"No, not really. I just thought that we had a dysfunctional family. But, you know, about six months ago, Odell commented that they didn't seem much like parents, never had." She looked at Davy and then at Andy. "Is that what you mean?"

"It might be. Odell may have suspected something." Davy opened the folder in front of him, closed it, opened it again and then looked up at Oshea.

Oshea watched him with a frown on her face. He wasn't acting normal, she thought.

"Davy? What is it? What did you discover?" Andy wrapped Oshea into a hug, feeling the shudders running through her.

"Burnie approached me this morning, asking me if we had considered that. He had been doing some research."

"He had?" Oshea glanced up at Andy, finding him frowning. "Andy?"

"It's okay. Burnie is a novelist and does a lot of research sometimes. That's what Davy meant. He would have been doing that for us."

"I see." Oshea moved away from the men, her thoughts troubled. *Is this why I have never felt like I belonged? That I had somehow known this all my life. I don't have any memories other than of them, and they're not the best at that.*

Chapter 29

Three days later, Oshea ran for the house, her breath coming in ragged gasps. She could hear the footsteps pounding across the grass after her. She fumbled for the door, through it, and then slamming it, the lock in place. She ran for the other doors, shoving the locks on, and then spun. Where was it Andy had told her to hide?

Oshea kept spinning before her eyes were on the master bedroom and she ran that way, scrambling for the latch at the back of the closet, pulling the hidden door open and then closed behind her, the bolt sliding in place to keep the door closed. She struggled to control her breathing, faintly hearing the sounds of breaking glass and then heavy footsteps on the hardwood floors. Sinking to the floor, she wrapped her arms around her knees, her face buried.

Andy stared at his house, at the broken open doors, and feared for Oshea. He struggled to release himself from Buckley's grip, watching in despair as Davy headed for the house, patrol officers fanning out to search.

"Was Oshea here?" Buckley's voice finally managed to get through Andy's terror.

"She was. Oh, please, dear Lord, let her be here. And safe." He watched as Davy holstered his weapon and headed his way. "Davy?"

"We don't see her, Andy, but that doesn't mean she isn't here. We're searching." He studied his young friend. "Where would she go?"

Andy began to shake his head and then was running for the house, not listening to Davy's words to stop. Davy was after him, tracking him to the bedroom. Finding the latch on the door, Andy tucked at it before he began pounding at it, his voice calling for Oshea.

Davy watched in amazement, before he reached to pull at Andy's arm. Andy shrugged him off, continuing to try and open the door. He heard a latch and then the door opened.

The banging and pounding on the door had startled Oshea, causing her to jump and scramble away from it, her eyes huge with her terror. Her heart had quickened as she heard Andy's calls for her and she scrambled back. Her fingers fumbled at the latch, missing it and then finally able to grasp it and pull it back. She pulled in turn at the door, cracking it open, finding Andy reaching for her and just enfolding her into his arms. He gathered her close, Davy's hands on his shoulder turning him from the closet and then shoving him out of the house and towards his car.

Sinking to the pavement in the shelter of the car, Andy just hugged Oshea tight. Her arms clung to his neck as sobs shook her body. Davy stood and watched, and then searched the area. He could feel someone near and that disturbed him. That was not what he wanted. Breck approached, concern colouring his face.

"Davy? What happened?" Breck stared down at Andy and Oshea, not sure how to approach them.

"Someone broke into their home. Oshea was able to hide. But we need to keep these two safe. Obviously being here doesn't." Davy excused himself as a patrol officer approached him and then walked around the house with him.

Breck crouched down beside Andy, a hand on his shoulder.

"Andy? Talk to me."

Andy looked up and Breck drew in a deep breath at the anger and fear that coloured his face.

"They were in our home, Breck. They tried to take Oshea from here. Where do we go?"

"Come back to the building, at least for now. You'll not be able to stay here right now."

Oshea loosened her arms enough to look up at Andy.

"They came in from the backyard, Andy. I ran. I didn't know where to hide at first."

"You did well, sweetheart. Hiding where I showed you." Andy just shook his head at Breck, not willing to state where it had been. "Did you get a look at them?"

Oshea shook her head and then leaned back against her groom.

"No. I just heard someone running towards me. I didn't think that I would make it in time. Did they break in?"

"They did, sweetheart. We'll have someone come in and repair everything." Andy stared up at Davy. "Davy's here. He needs to hear what you said. Then, we'll move back to the building. At least for now."

Davy crouched down beside them, Breck moving away, his phone out to call Barnabas.

"Barnabas?" Breck could hear the paper shuffling as Barnabas searched for something. "Someone tried to nab Oshea at their home. I'm bringing them back to the building."

"They did? We wondered if that would happen. Okay. I think the suite that Oshea had used is the best one. Has anyone said where the investigation stands?"

"Not that I am aware of. Andy hasn't said. This is frustrating, Barnabas. And he said that her brother is missing."

"He is? We have someone looking for him?"

"We do. I'll call with a head's up when we leave. Someone will need to shop for them."

"Cadee's around. I'll talk to her and she'll find someone to go with her."

Breck pocketed his phone, walking back towards Andy, finding him on his feet, Oshea standing beside him, an expression of her face that Breck could just not describe.

"Breck? We're ready to go." Andy grasped Oshea's hand, pulling with him, wondering why she just didn't move. He turned to her, to find her staring away from him.

Oshea pulled away from Andy, her feet carrying her towards a man standing by himself before she was running towards him, throwing herself at him. Davy was on the move, running rapidly after her, not in time to prevent the man from catching her to him. Andy was there almost as soon as Oshea, his hand up to draw her away until he stared at the man.

"Andy?" Breck was beside him, a hand on his shoulder.

"It's her brother. Odell. I thought that he was missing. That's what Davy said."

Chapter 30

Davy stared at the younger man, before he turned, beckoning over a patrol officer. This was not what he had expected. How had Odell managed to arrive there? And was he part of the group that had just tried to abduct Oshea? Hard questions were coming his way, that much Davy knew.

"Davy, we need to get the three out of here." Breck's voice was low. "I spoke with Barnabas. Andy and Oshea are moving back to the building. I suggest that we take her brother as well, if that really is him."

"It's him. Head that way. I'll send a couple of patrol vehicles with you." Davy walked away, turning to watch Oshea.

Oshea stepped back, finding Andy tight behind her. Her eyes were on her brother, seeing how unkempt and fatigued he was.

"Odell?"

Odell shook his head. "Not now, Oshea. We need to find somewhere safe. This was part of trying to get you."

Breck moved in, nodding at Andy.

"We're moving out of here now. Andy?"

"With you, Breck. Sweetheart, come. Now. Breck wants to move us out of here as does Davy. We're not safe."

"No, we're not. And I am not leaving Odell." Oshea was digging in her heels. Andy gave a swift grin at that.

"No, we won't leave him. Breck has made arrangements for us to go back to the building."

Oshea stared at him and then at Breck before a shuttered look covered her face. She sighed. *Lord, didn't we just leave there? How can we heal if we go back? How do we move forward? How does Andy reclaim his life and fly for You once more?*

Odell had his eyes on Davy before he looked down at his sister.

"Oshea? I'm sorry. I didn't know that was what was planned. I need to talk to the police. Let me know where you'll be. I'll find you."

Davy reached out a hand to steady him.

"I'm Davy. I'm the investigator here and I've been looking for you. Go with your sister for now, but don't say another word. I'll be here for a while and then I'll find you.

Brady and Brody stood watching as Oshea and Andy walked towards them, Breck following with Odell. They exchanged glances before Brody nodded.

"Her brother, I suspect."

"How did he get here? I thought he was missing."

"That he was. But I think Brendon had a lead on him or was it Benen?"

"No, it was Baird. This changes it, you know."

Breck shook his head as he passed them, knowing that he would track them down later. Brady and Brody stared at one another and then after the four before they headed for Brody's vehicle, intent on the lead that they were following.

Oshea stood once more in the suite that she had vacated not that many days earlier. She could hear Breck and Andy speaking with one another but her focus was on her brother, who sat with his head in his hands. Doc appeared, summoned by Breck.

"Oshea? I heard you had some trouble earlier? You're okay?" He grinned as she snorted.

"Okay would be a relative word, now wouldn't it? I'm fine. I didn't get hurt, just terrified once more. Do you have a cure for that?"

Doc shook a finger at her even as he turned to her brother.

"And who do we have here?"

"My brother, Odell. He was missing, Doc. Please? Can you check him out?"

"I can do that, if he'll let me. I know Davy will want a report." Doc studied the younger man before he had him on his feet, heading for the infirmary. "I'll take him downstairs, Oshea. Once we're done, then

I'll bring him back up, if Davy hasn't appeared by that time."

Andy watched as the two men walked away before he turned to Oshea. Breck's eyes were on them both before he sighed. *How do we do this, Lord? How do we keep them safe? Having Odell here has just increased her danger and vulnerability.*

"Oshea? Talk to me." Breck approached her, finding her not responding. "Andy?"

"I know, Breck. Oshea?" His voice reached through the fog that she had been under.

"Andy? Where did he come from? Is he part of this all?" Oshea was suddenly deeply afraid. "I know he looks rough, but how are we to be around him until we know?"

Davy had appeared as she spoke, his head shaking at Breck.

"Oshea?" He waited until she looked at him. "We hear what you're saying. Odell was definitely abducted. Why and how he showed up at your place? That we will discuss with him. For now, we keep him here, away from town, and try to keep all three of you safe. If we can."

"That's the rub, isn't it, Davy? How do you keep us all safe?" Oshea walked away on those words, out of the door, leaving the three men staring at one another.

Chapter 31

Sitting on the side of the bed in the infirmary, knowing Doc was working away behind him, Odell looked up as he heard footsteps. He frowned, not knowing who was walking his way. Then he sighed. This was getting old, he thought.

"Odell? I'm Davy. I'm the one investigating what's going on with your sister and her husband." Davy watched him intently.

"Her husband? She's not married. She's not dating." Odell was puzzled at Davy's words. "The last I heard was that she was missing."

"Yes, she went missing. Kidnapped and then forced onto a plane. A plane that Andy was intending to use on his vacation. Only he never got to that. His plane went down not far from her. Oshea's kidnapper disappeared but we have him in custody. And your sister is married to Andy. That is a step they took just a few days ago. Now, about you." His pad of paper and pen were out. "Talk to me, Odell. Tell me what happened. Leave nothing out. There are men around here who would be very upset if you're doing this to hurt your sister."

"I'm not!" Odell was horrified at the thought. "I thought that if I left town, I could talk her into going with me. I quit my job, gave up my apartment, but when I went to find her, I couldn't. She wasn't there. No one seemed to know where she was. I couldn't ask our parents. They were too busy, just like always."

"When were you abducted?"

"As I was leaving my apartment. I had gone to Oshea's apartment and hadn't found her. When I went back to my own apartment and packed up and then turned to go down the stairs, two men were there." Odell's face hardened for a moment. "They forced me to go with them, threatening Oshea to make me. I thought that they had her somewhere. They treated me roughly. I wasn't given much to eat or drink. Then, they made me go to that house." His brow wrinkled for a moment. "I heard them saying something about Oshea. When I was left alone with just one of them, I managed to slug him and then disappear. I hid, not knowing where to go. I saw Oshea when she came out of the house. That's when you found me."

"Can you describe the men?"

"Not really. I was blindfolded before I knew what was happening. Their voices kept changing. I think they were trying to discuss them. There were at least three, that much I know. And I don't know where I was kept. But it wasn't in our hometown. We drove away from there the day that they took me." Odell studied his hands, frowning at how he was shaking. "I'm sorry. I'm not much help."

"No, it's fine. It is what it is." Davy shared a look with Doc. "Now, about your parents. What can you tell me about their business?"

"Their business. They have a lot of different businesses. I worked in their one department, but I left there. Something was off about it all. Dad had become more secretive, meeting men and women outside of office hours. This is new for him. When I asked him about it, he just shrugged it off. Something about a merger with another company and they had to meet outside of office hours. Only he would never say what business. That fact disturbed me. Mom wouldn't say much either. She was the head of their overseas department, looking after their exports and imports. Only there didn't seem to be much there anymore. I know they had laid off personnel in it, but she said it was only temporary. Just until they could finish their reorganization. Only that never happened either."

"It sounds as if your parents were hiding something." Davy looked down and then back at Odell. "For now, Odell, you are to stay here. I've arranged for you to have a suite here. There is security on site. Doc here will look after you."

"That's right, Odell. Here, let's get you to your suite. Tonight? You sleep. I know that Anna, my wife, has fixed food for you." Doc didn't give Odell a choice, merely moving him from the room and to his suite.

Davy stood in the lobby, lost in thought, looking up as Barnabas and Bradon approached, Bradon's dog, Kade, pacing with them.

"Davy? Odell getting settled?" Barnabas was uncertain about having him there, not knowing how he fit into the situation.

"He is. Doc is looking after him. Watch him, Barnabas. Until we can confirm his story, it is a risk to have him here."

"We'll do that. Andy said that he would try and keep Oshea separate from him. She's uncertain as well about him."

"I picked that up. Listen, I have to run. I've been called into another investigation." Davy was gone before they could say anything more.

"Just how serious is he about Odell?" Bradon's hand rested on Kade's head.

"Very, I would say. Did you fellows find out anything about him?"

"Not a whole lot. Emma was going to look into it but she and Jace were tied up on a search that they could not put aside." Bradon was frustrated.

"That happens, Bradon. Off with you now. I know you were heading out."

"I was, but I think I'll stay put. Something is off and I don't know what."

"I know what you're meaning. I'm heading to check with Doc and then Andy. Call me if you need me." Barnabas walked away, leaving Bradon and Kade to pace the lobby.

Chapter 32

Two days later, Oshea paced the lobby. She had spoken with Odell that morning and was feeling unsettled. Something just wasn't ringing true, she thought. What he is saying is so different from what he said. What changed with that? Andy was away, at another doctor's appointment. She prayed that this time, he would be cleared to fly. He needed that, she decided. It was who he was.

Cadee hesitated to approach Oshea until Oshea turned and smiled. She walked towards her, reaching out to hug her.

"Oshea? You're free? Where's Andy?"

"He's off for an appointment. They wouldn't let me go with him. Right at the moment, I am at loose ends and feeling somewhat lost."

Cadee laughed and then linked an arm with Oshea.

"I was heading to find you. We're meeting in the other conference room. Just us ladies. We try and meet once a week for prayer. We can do that, but we want to help you."

146

"And just how would you do that?" Oshea stopped just inside the door, finding the room decorated. "Cadee? What's going on?"

"This is for you, Oshea. We understand where you're at. You know all of our stories. We've regaled you with them." Imly danced up to hug her. "Now, it's your turn. We want to give to you, to welcome you to our family. It's huge, I know, but you're such a welcome part of it. Andy has been there for us."

Oshea looked around and then moved to hug each of the ladies, Anna and Amy included. The twins were there too, eager to get the party going as they stated. The ladies laughed at them.

Later that afternoon, Oshea drew a deep breath, tears sparkling in her eyes as she stared at the gifts that she had been given. Her hand reached for the Bible that the twins and Darby had given her. She missed hers and had been reluctant to ask Andy for one. She felt arms around her and leaned back against him.

"You're home, Andy. Have you been for long?"

"Not too long. I was meeting with Barnabas and Bruce when I got back." Andy waited for her to speak.

"Your appointment? How did it go?"

"It went fine. The doctor thinks another couple of weeks and then he'll do the physical that I need. He doesn't seem to think there will be any issues." Andy's chin rested on her shoulder. "Been shopping without me?"

Oshea's head shook. "No, the ladies had a shower for me, if you can believe that. Just to welcome me to the family, they said. They are so wonderful."

Andy's finger touched the leather cover on the Bible.

"You're holding this." He groaned. "You didn't have one. I never thought, sweetheart."

"It's okay, Andy. I have now." She stared down at the gifts. "I never expected this, you know."

"No, you wouldn't. It's what they do. The family just opens up and takes in whoever is next to come." Andy turned her to face him. "I spoke with Davy today."

"Did you? What did he have to say?" She was hopeful that their adventure was almost over.

"He's working through a lot of material, and has a number of cases that he has to deal with. Will Peters was also around. He's concerned about Odell."

"I am too. He's different, Andy, than he used to be. I'm not sure what to make of it."

"That we've been picking up. Davy is heading towards your town, he tells me, with search warrants for both of your apartments. We'll need to go there soon as well."

"Yeah, there's that." Oshea suddenly hugged Andy, just holding on to him. "I'm scared, Andy. This isn't over. I don't want anyone hurt."

"We know that. And before you ask, any letters that have come have gone directly to Davy. They're not letting us see them. So far, there haven't been any parcels."

"That's good, I guess. What are we to do? I know. I keep repeating myself."

"We all do. Sweetheart, what are you planning on doing once this is all behind us?"

"I'm not sure what you're meaning." Oshea frowned, causing Andy to reach and kiss her. She snuggled closer to him.

"For work."

"That I don't know, Andy. Why?"

"It's just that we need to talk about finances. You know that the Foundation pays me. When we married, you became an employee of the Foundation. As my wife, you receive a salary from them. That means you can either work, go to school, stay at home, or volunteer. We explained that the Foundation pays wages so that the employers are free to hire other staff."

"You did. I just didn't expect it to happen to me." Oshea was lost in thought. "So, that means I don't have to rush to make a decision."

"Not at all. We'll get this behind us and then go forward." Andy groaned as his phone rang. This was not a good time, he thought, pulling it out. He pulled up the text messages, paling as he read them before he sent them on to Davy.

"Threats, Andy?" Oshea leaned against him. "Oh, my. They are not nice, are they?"

"Not at all. You haven't had any?"

"No, but then only you and the ones here have my number. And Davy. Dallas asked me about that too."

"He did? He will. He'll have some good ideas for us. In fact, we need to brainstorm with him."

Oshea smirked at him. "Then, I guess it's a good thing that I asked them for a meal." She glanced at the clock. "They'll be here in an hour. That gives me time to finish off the meal." She waited for Andy to let go of her. "Andy?"

He grinned at her. "That also gives me time to kiss and cuddle with my sweetheart for a few moments."

Chapter 33

Dallas took the mug of coffee offered to him with thanks, hesitating for a moment before he sat in the living room with Andy. He could hear Deri and Oshea in the kitchen, their soft laughter wafting their way. He was afraid for his friend and his lady, knowing what they were facing.

"Andy? Where does the investigation stand?"

Andy shrugged. "I have no idea at the moment. Davy's not saying much. I'm starting to get the text messages that always come."

"I wondered. Sent them on?"

"I have." Andy rubbed at his face. "How did you do it? You went through so much, even as a police officer."

"We did. God got us through, Andy. And that's not some trite flippant remark. I don't know how people without faith make it through. We had support from here, from Deri's family. My own brother and sister wanted to be here, but we kept them isolated to protect them."

"I remember. Oshea is not seeing her parents. In fact, her father has been arrested. Her brother is here but not in a lot of contact with her. Davy is seeing to that. It's hard for her."

"It is. What can we do to help?" Dallas watched Andy closely, seeing the ladies coming in to sit with them.

"Why would you ask that, Dallas?" Oshea was puzzled.

"It's what we do, Oshea. I'm a retired detective."

"I understand that. I just don't get what you're asking."

Andy sighed, wrapping an arm around Oshea. He puzzled how to explain it to her.

"It's like this, Oshea. Davy and the police are working away, trying to investigate but they can't be with us all the time. Dallas is wanting to help, to make plans with us."

"Oh, I see." Oshea's gaze had not left Dallas. "What do you suggest?"

Dallas shared a look with Deri before he began to speak. His words hit home with the younger couple, Andy nodding at times. Oshea was troubled. She really didn't think what he had suggested would work.

Andy watched Oshea later that night. He sighed to himself. *This is not going well, Lord. How do we do this? How do we keep us safe and still grow together as a couple and in our faith?*

"Andy?" He turned as Oshea spoke to him. "Will this work?"

"I have no idea. Dallas has made suggestions for us that it is up to us whether we follow or not, but it's contingent on the other side. And we have no idea what they are planning."

"That's what frightens me." Oshea frowned. "Did you say if we have received parcels of any kind?"

"Not that I am aware of. I'm told about the letters but not parcels. Why?"

"Aren't we supposed to be getting them?"

"We are but somehow we're not. I know I have been followed when I've been out." Andy paused, realizing that he had been out but not Oshea. "Oshea, we need to get you out and about."

"We do? Is it safe?" Her face lit up at the thought.

"Not likely, but you need to do this. We need to do this. I'll be back at work in a couple of weeks and you can't just sit around here."

"We need to move back home, Andy. I can't stay here." Oshea dropped her eyes, not wanting to see him refuse.

"I know we do. We'll do that. Tomorrow." Andy wrapped in his arms. "Dad and Mom want us to come for a meal. Would tomorrow night work?"

Oshea nodded, a sober look on her face. "But we'll be putting them in danger."

"It doesn't matter if we're around them or not. If whoever it is wants to, they'll go after them."

"I know." Oshea leaned against him, drawing from his strength. "Andy, where is God in all this?" Her question was one that didn't need an answer. She just had to vocalize it.

Chapter 34

Andy's knees and hands hit the concrete floor of the hangar, a groan drawn from him. He had not seen the men running towards him nor heard them, the sound of the plane engine drowning out their footsteps. He was hauled to his feet, his face contorted with pain. He shook his head, regretting it at the pounding that ensued, not hearing what he was asked. He was finally left in a heap, his hand rubbing at his face and the other hand at his back,

Sitting up gingerly, Andy looked around. He was alone. How do they keep getting in, he asked himself. They shouldn't be but they are. His walk steadied as he moved to the plane, heading up the stairs and to the cockpit. He had been cleared to fly, and for that he was grateful. God had healed him and heard their prayers. Andy was due to fly out that afternoon, heading across the province and back with Bruce and Barnabas. It was an overnight flight and he hated to leave Oshea on her own.

Barnabas' eyes were on Andy as he seated himself in the cockpit, knowing that his father had buckled himself into a seat in the cabin. He waited patiently, knowing that Andy would speak when he felt he was free to.

"Andy? What happened?" Barnabas just finally had to ask.

"The men again. How do they keep getting into the hangar?" Andy was frustrated and that frustration came out in a bite in his words.

"Again? When?" Barnabas was disturbed, to say the least.

"About an hour ago. They took me down and then left. I have no idea what it is that they are after."

"That's what's frustrating us all. We can't get a sense of what it is that they are after."

"And Oshea has no idea. I've talked with Odell. He doesn't either. Or else he's not saying. He's a hard read, Barnabas."

"I know." Barnabas became silent, his mind whirling at the possibilities. "I think that we need to speak with Darcy Foster."

"Darcy?"

"She's a retired forensics psychologist. She can read him for us. I asked Davy about that just this morning. He was agreeable and would be reaching out to her."

"I wish this was over." Andy didn't continue but he didn't need to. Barnabas understood to a certain extent how he felt. *Lord, please be with my friends. Guide us as we investigate. Protect them. Help us to solve this quickly.*

Andy moved quickly the next morning, heading for his home. Oshea had called him just as he was landing and he hadn't been able to talk with her for long. The door swung open under his hand and he paused.

"Oshea?" He didn't hear her and began his search. "Oshea?"

He didn't find her and began a more systematic search. He stood on the front walk, staring at his home, devastation on his face. She had disappeared, and he had no idea where she was.

Oshea ran as hard and as fast as she could towards him. She had been home when she heard a sound at the door and ran from her home, seeking safety. The senior neighbour had watched and then beckoned her to come towards her. Oshea had been grateful for her assistance but worried about Glory's safety. Glory had merely shrugged and stated that no one would know that she was there. She had then simply picked up the phone and called for help.

Andy turned slightly as he heard the footsteps, finding Oshea throwing herself at him. The patrol officer moved them away from the house as the area was searched.

"Andy?" Davy spoke from beside them. "What happened?"

"I don't know. I flew back in this morning, came home, and didn't find Oshea in the house." Andy stared down at his bride. "Oshea? What happened?"

"They did. Again. When will it stop?" The men could ear the anger in her voice.

"They didn't find you. Where did you go?" Davy turned a circle, trying to see whereabouts it was that she had hidden.

"Your neighbour, Glory. She helped me, Andy. I just hope that they don't find out that she did." Oshea was tired suddenly, the release of the stress that she had been under that day causing her to slump towards the ground.

Andy gave a sound and just gathered her up, turning to head for his car. Davy was beside them, reaching to open the door for Andy. He watched the crowd that had gathered before he was away, yelling for an officer to help. Andy watched for a moment before his attention went back to Oshea.

"Oshea? What happened?"

"Someone was looking for me again, Andy. I ran and Glory helped me." She looked up at him. "But how was your day? You made good time."

"We did. A successful trip, Bruce said." Andy crouched down beside her, his hands reaching for hers. "What are we to do?"

Oshea shrugged, a small smile crossing her face.

"I have no idea." She looked up as Davy approached. "And here is Davy back."

Chapter 35

The men in the conference room looked up as Breck appeared, sheaves of paper in his hand. They had pulled back from their work, trying their best to solve this for Andy and Oshea. Only it was going nowhere. None of them had been able to figure it out.

"Breck?" Benen's voice caught Breck's attention. "What are we missing?"

"Something, Benen. Only I don't know what." Breck sighed. "And now we have this. This is not directly related to either Andy or Oshea but there are hints in here that it is. Bruce was emailed this information. We need to take a look at it and see what we have." He looked around. "If we don't make progress in the next day or so, you'll need to go back to your work, as hard as it is to do that."

The men nodded before they bent over their tasks. Breck looked around, finding Buckley beside him.

"What can we do for them, Breck, that we're not already?"

"That I'm not sure of, Buckley. This doesn't make a lot of sense." Breck was puzzled.

"It never has. We don't understand how they keep getting to the hangar. Andy said that he was assaulted again there."

"I know. That's what Barnabas said." Breck rubbed at his face. "Buckley, what are your thoughts?"

"My thoughts? That we are being played and played big time. Oshea and Odell don't seem to fit with their parents, but we can't find any evidence that they're not their biological children. We can't find the evidence that her parents are not on the up and up, that they're criminals." Buckley paused his words, before he pointed at Breck. "That's what we're doing wrong. We're trying to prove that they are criminals. We need to prove that they're not."

Breck stared at him, before looking past him at Brendon and Brandon standing there, nodding in agreement.

"That's what we've been working on, Breck." Brendon shared a look with Brandon. "We didn't think it made sense." He handed over a file. "This is what we've found. There is a silent partner in their firms. And he has a known association to criminal families. But I can't see them not knowing that."

"I wonder?" Breck reached for the file, opening it and scanning it. "Good work, fellows. Now, we talk to Davy and see what he has to say"

"Wait, Breck, before you do. We need to do some more on that." Brennen had approached. "Let's work away on that assumption, see what we find. I volunteer to talk with Oshea. Someone needs to talk with Odell."

Oshea stared at Brennen and then at Brandon.

"I don't understand what you're saying." She was puzzled as to what they were asking.

"We've discovered that your parents had a silent partner in their firms. He's a known connection to a criminal family. Do you recognize this man?" Brennen handed over a photo.

Oshea drew a deep breath before she looked down at the photo.

"No, I don't know him. But I didn't work there. In fact, I was hardly there. Most of their meetings were off site or after hours." She bit at her lip. "Are you saying that they're criminals?"

"No, not necessarily." Brandon spoke up. "We're working it both ways. Trying to prove that they are and trying to prove that they're not."

Oshea was confused. "That's a strange way to do things."

Andy gave a low laugh. "It's what they do, sweetheart. They try and find the evidence that they need. And they do. Each one looks at it differently." He grinned suddenly. "How far ahead of you are the ladies?"

Brennen and Brandon both grinned.

"They're working it. We haven't heard yet, but I'm sure that we will." Brennen paused, a thought crossing his mind. "Oshea, call us if you think of anything at all."

"I will. You said someone was speaking with Odell?"

"They are." Brandon stared at her. "Your names are unusual, do you know that?"

"They are. We were never given an explanation for them, no matter how much we asked. We often wondered if they were surnames but we could never find out."

Andy nodded, his eyes narrowing as he thought about what they had said. He sighed to himself as he closed the door behind Brandon and Brennen. Oshea was watching him before she walked away. This was just getting so strange, he thought. How did they find out what was going on without more danger coming to them?

Chapter 36

Two weeks had passed with no clear resolution to their mystery. Both Andy and Oshea were frustrated. They knew that God was in control and that He would work it all out for them, but they still worried about one another. Andy was back flying as much as he had been, working with the Foundation Board to set up for flight instruction. He was excited about that opportunity, something that he had wanted to do for years, but concerned about the students.

Oshea, on the other hand, had no idea what she wanted to do. She researched different areas of employment, talked with the building ladies and Andy's mother, but had no clear route ahead of her to follow. Like Andy, she was afraid for those around her that might be harmed. She had had long talks with Odell, but neither one of them had answers.

Bradon worked away that day, alone in the conference room, Kade on his bed near him. He rose, a puzzled look on his face and approached the whiteboards. Nodding, he turned, a hand on Kade's head.

"Is this it, boy? Is this the answer? I need to speak with Oshea. Now, where would she be?" He walked away, the lights off in the room and the door locked, Kade pacing beside him. Bradon's face lit up as he saw Ennis walking towards him, Oshea at her side. He reached to hug his wife. "I didn't expect to see you today. I thought that you were off on a trip somewhere."

"I was going to, but Oshea called. She wanted to talk with one of you. And you won." Ennis' grin lit up her face.

Bradon turned to Oshea, a frown momentarily crossing his face. *She's troubled, isn't she, Lord. And what can I do to help?*

"Oshea? You wanted to talk with us?"

"I do." Oshea's arms were wrapped around herself, a defensive measure Bradon thought. "Where do we stand with the investigation? I feel like it is going nowhere. Davy has had to set it aside even though he hasn't wanted to. He said he has no new information. Andy has spoken with Emma and Jace and even they can't help."

Bradon nodded. It was what they had all expected.

"Actually, I was coming to find you. If you hadn't appeared here, Kade and I were heading for your home." He turned back to the conference room. "In here, I think. First, Oshea, let's pray. I do have some information and names that I need to run by you."

———

Raising his head, Bradon shared a look with Ennis. *This is it, isn't it,* he thought. *This is where I have to lay it on the line for her. Only I don't know where it will take us.* He looked around as the door opened and Buckley and Locklin appeared, coming to find seats near them. He never quite understood how Buckley knew exactly when and where he was needed but he knew God was leading there.

"Bradon? What did you find?" Oshea's voice was barely audible. She wanted, no needed Andy here, but he was away that day with some of the Foundation board at a meeting north of where they lived.

"Oshea, I have found some information. How it applies to you, I'm not quite sure." Bradon studied his paperwork before he handed it over. "I have been looking at your parents' family. Did you know that you have aunts and uncles outside of the province?"

Oshea shook her head. "That can't be right. We were always told that they were only children. This is proof of that?" At Bradon's nod, she sighed. "If they lied about this, what else did they lie about? Have you contacted them?"

"No, I will leave that for Davy. I have sent him the material. And Micah's wife, Kataleen, has been working with her family tree program and told me that she would forward what information that she could to him as well. I'm sorry, Oshea. This is not what you needed to hear."

"No, I think we do need to hear this. It just doesn't make sense." Oshea flipped through the papers, reading the names. "I have never heard of any of these people. What did they do? Are we originally here from Ontario?"

"That's what your birth certificates state. That you were born here. Only we're not sure on that at all."

"You think that we were adopted? And that we're from out of the province?" Oshea was on her feet, pacing. "I don't understand, Bradon. Why would they do that?"

"That's what Brendon and Branigan were working on, I think. It may mean that they have to fly out of the province." Bradon's hand went up. "We've done it before. We have no proof, as yet, of this. That's where our research comes in."

"I see." Oshea stared at the floor, her emotions mixed. "Has someone spoken with Odell about this?"

"Not yet. I just finalized my work." Bradon shared a look with Buckley who simply shook his head. Oshea would need time to absorb his findings and needed time to discuss it with Andy. "I plan on doing that, Oshea. Just know that we are trying our best to figure it all out for you."

"I know." Her words were barely audible. "I just wish that it was different." She was on her feet, walking away from them, leaving the two men standing and staring after her.

———

Chapter 37

Andy's parents stood at their doorway, his father's hand raised to knock once more before he stepped back from the porch. Walking around the house, he searched, not seeing either Andy or Oshea. His hand rested on the knob to the back door, finding it turning under his hand. Andy's mother, Sarah, watched from the patio.

"It's unlocked?"

"It is, Sarah." Stephen stood back on the patio beside her before he pulled out his phone. "We need to call the police, Sarah. I can't just walk in."

"No, you can't." They walked back around to the front of the house, leaning against their car. "Have they disappeared?"

"They knew that we were coming today." Stephen watched as a patrol car approached, feeling for his phone. "They said that they would be here."

The officer approached them, a frown on his face.

"Andy?"

"He's not answering. Neither is Oshea. They were expecting us." Stephen nodded towards the door. "The front door is locked. The back door isn't. I tried the knob but didn't go in. We called you instead."

"Ok. Stay right here. I'll take a look." The officer approached the front of the house, repeating the steps that Stephen and Sarah had taken.

They stood and watched as he searched, disappearing around the house. His arm around his wife, Stephen prayed for his son, knowing that if they were there, they couldn't answer. But his heart told him otherwise. They were not in the house. He began to pray, petitioning and pleading for his son's safety and that of Oshea. Sarah trembled in his arms, struggling to control emotions.

Breck paused as he and Branigan walked towards the house. Branigan had found him, insistent that they needed to go to Andy's home. Something was wrong, he had simply stated. Breck had stared at him and then nodded, heading for a vehicle.

"Stephen?" Breck's quiet voice startled Stephen, whose head jerked around. "What's going on?"

"They're missing, Breck. At least, we think they are. We arrived as we said we would. Only they're not answering. An officer is searching right now." He peered at the two men. "That doesn't explain why you two are here."

"I felt something this morning, Stephen. A warning, I guess you could say. I hunted down Breck and we headed here. I was that worried about them."

Branigan watched the older couple and then raised his eyes to where the patrol officer stood by his car. "He's calling in help."

"That would be my guess." Breck turned in a circle, searching the area. "We're being watched."

"We are?" Sarah sighed. "That's what they always do, don't they? They make whoever it is disappear and then stand and watch the search and the distress that the friends and families are put through."

Breck gave a grim smile at that before he stepped away, his phone out. He turned it over and over in his hands, knowing that he had to call Barnabas. Instead, he called Buckley.

"Buckley? We have a situation here. I know that I need to call Daniel, but Andy's a part of our family. It appears that he and Oshea are missing."

"Missing?" Buckley was on his feet, heading away from his office on a search for Locklin. "Who discovered that?"

"His parents. They were to meet today. Only Andy and Oshea are not here. And yes, they did call it in. Officers are here now. But can you come?" Breck turned to watch Andy's parents, nodding as Branigan looked his way. "Branigan's here but I would appreciate it if you two would come."

"We're on our way." Buckley pocketed his phone as he reached for Locklin's hand.

"Andy's?" Locklin's voice held the fear that she felt.

"That's right. They're missing."

———

Barnabas was on a hunt after he had spoken with Breck. Dismayed at the turn of events, he needed to find Bruce and put into place a plan of some kind. Only he had no idea what kind of plan that would be. He knew some of the men were in the conference room and that their ladies were as well.

Not finding his father, Barnabas stood for a moment, a hand on the conference room door before he opened it. He was not surprised to find all the men there and their ladies as well, working away as they always did. He glanced at the whiteboards and nodded. Progress, he thought, had been made, but would it help?

A few quiet words with the men and ladies and then Bradon was on his feet, Kade pacing beside him as he headed for the door. He would search, he informed Barnabas, as he always did. He would not interfere in the investigation, that much was certain, but he knew that he would be of aid to that very investigation.

Chapter 38

Will Peters approached Breck, a frown on his face. He had just been informed of the situation. He knew that Davy was heading that way at some point. Breck turned as his friend neared him.

"They're gone, Will." Breck was disheartened, his eyes on Andy's parents as they stood with Buckley and Locklin. Branigan was around somewhere, and he had seen Bradon and Kade moving in to help search.

"That's what I have been told. Stephen found that out?"

"He did. They were to be here this morning, he said. Andy told him late last night that he didn't have to fly anywhere today and that they would be home. Only, they're not."

"I see. Stay with Stephen and Sarah. I'll be back." Will walked away and towards Davy, who had arrived. "Davy?"

"This is frustrating, Will. I just got word from the street that someone was looking for them. And this is the result?" Davy rubbed at his temple, a headache starting that he really didn't need.

———

171

"Unfortunately, it is." Will searched the area, his gaze coming to rest on Sarah. "They're hurting, Davy. Do what you need to. I'm heading back in for a meeting, but update me, please."

Davy watched Will disappear and then headed for the house, his conversation with the crime scene techs short. He sighed. No evidence of where they are. They wouldn't have just walked away or at least he didn't think that they would. He eventually made his way towards Stephen and Sarah, not as familiar with them as he should be, he thought.

"Stephen. Sarah. Andy and Oshea were definitely to be here this morning?"

"They were." Stephen sighed, not sure where his son had gotten to. "We spoke late last evening. They had no plans to go anywhere today, he said. He didn't have anything booked and Oshea was not planning on shopping, he said."

Davy nodded, his eyes on Sarah.

"Sarah?" His voice brought her eyes to him. "What can you add? You look puzzled and troubled."

"I am, Davy." Sarah rubbed at her arms. "I had a long talk with Oshea yesterday. She stopped by in the afternoon. She is puzzled about her brother and said he wasn't acting like he usually did. She just couldn't put a finger on what was different. And that concerns me. Is he involved?"

"Not that we are aware of. He's been moved elsewhere for now, just to protect both himself and

Oshea. I can't go into any details about that." Davy frowned for a moment. "What else, Sarah?"

"We talked about her parents. She said she had to talk to someone. Oshea is really confused right now about them. She's reached out but they haven't really responded. She stated that sometimes they were like that and sometimes they responded quickly. I got the impression that this was how it had been all her life. With Odell around, she felt somewhat secure she said but not totally. She had promised me that she would talk it over with Andy again. Oshea and Andy have discussed this more than once, we know, but neither of them seem to have a sense of what's going on there. Do you?"

"We're beginning to, Sarah, but there are a lot of false leads and misinformation that we're discovering."

"That doesn't sound good." Stephen spoke up, his eyes on Breck, who nodded. "I know that you're needing to be off somewhere else, Davy. Call us when you can, just to keep us updated. We're going to be searching as well."

"I am sure that you will be. Just stay safe. If you find anything or hear anything, I want to know. You are not to go in on your own. Understand?" Davy kept an eye on them until they nodded. He shook his head as he walked away, certain that they would not do that. That worried him, to put it mildly.

Breck approached them after having stepped away to take a call.

"Barnabas has asked if you two would come out to the building. The men and ladies are working away but would like to speak with you and more importantly, pray with you both."

Stephen and Sarah shared a look.

"We can do that, Breck. We appreciate it."

"Okay, then. Why don't you and Buckley's head out? I need to find Branigan and then we'll follow."

Breck watched them walk away, Bradon appearing at his side.

"Bradon? Talk to me."

"Nothing, Breck. Kade followed them to the driveway and then lost them. I think they were walked out and then taken away. There is no sign of any struggle, not from what I overheard."

"So they knew who it was or else one of them was threatened."

"I would say Oshea was threatened." Bradon shared a look with Branigan. "If it had been Andy, Oshea would likely have gone along but we would have seen signs of a struggle. There's just not that."

"No? I suspect you're right. You're done here?"

"I am, Breck. I'm heading back for the building. Something is puzzling me about all this and I have a thought that I want to run with." Bradon grimaced, thinking of his friends. "I have reached out to Emma and Jace with it. Hopefully, they'll have something that I can work with."

"Go on, then. We'll be along shortly." Breck waited, knowing that Branigan was mulling something over. "Branigan?"

"If it had been her parents, would she have gone with them?" Branigan jammed his hands into his jacket pocket. "I suspect that she would have, but would Andy?"

"That's a good question, Branigan. What made you think of that?" Breck knew how Branigan thought.

"God, I guess. It's not making sense that a stranger would have taken them without some kind of a protest or reaction. If it was someone whom one of them knew, then I could see them going. Maybe saying that someone was hurt and needed them."

Breck nodded. "I suspect it's something like that. Let's head off, Branigan. You'll be wanting to work that."

Chapter 39

A week passed and then a second one. There had been no sightings of either Andy or Oshea. When questioned, Odell had stared at the investigator who had approached him at Davy's request and simply shaken his head. He had no idea, he stated, where his sister was. And why would they think that, he questioned?

The building men had been searching the town and surrounding area, with no results. The ladies had taken to spending much time in prayer, petitioning God for their friends, for their safety and for their return to them. Buckley and Locklin had shared a look and then sat down, their heads together in planning. Locklin had sighed and asked Buckley just what they were trying to accomplish anyway.

Stephen and Sarah had searched as well, with no success. He had taken to driving by Andy's home and just sitting, staring at the house, willing his son to come back.

There had been no ransom demand, no photos appearing of either Andy or Oshea, no threats directed at their families if they didn't cooperate. These facts had everyone puzzled. Davy had sat one morning, his thoughts muddled, before he had risen, found Will, and presented him with a plan. Will had questioned him at length and then sent him on his way. Davy had disappeared from the detachment, changed, and then appeared on the streets again, back to where he had spent so many months. He felt it might be the only way that he could or would find them.

The people on the street were surprised to see Davy reappear, knowing that he was an officer. Why was he back, they questioned? When they were told about Andy and Oshea, looks had been exchanged, and then Davy could see the determination in the faces to find the couple. Only, no one had seen him. There was no word on the streets about them. That puzzled everyone. Just where were they? And were they even still alive? That was the question that everyone was avoiding, not wanting to face the reality that they weren't.

Barnabas stood one more, just after the two-week mark, and stared at the building. Where are they, Lord? Why have we no word on them? I just pray that they aren't dead. He turned as he heard a vehicle, frowning at the SUV that approached.

Abe Finlay dropped to the ground. He had come specifically to speak with Barnabas.

"Abe? You're here? Where's Emma? And your team?" Barnabas approached him.

"Emma's caught up in a rush investigation, but she sent some material for her. My guys are training today." Abe looked around. "Any word?"

"Not a one." Barnabas stood, arms folded across his chest. "And that's frustrating and worrying."

"It is. I'm surprised that you haven't heard anything." Abe studied the other man.

———

"And Davy's been on the street without any word. That's unusual." Barnabas pointed to the building. "How be we go in and take a look at what the guys are working on? The ladies have been helping. They all want to find Andy and Oshea. Andy's a quiet one but he's been a support in many ways."

"I know he has. We've talked, Andy and I, many times. This is where it is hard to have faith and trust in God."

"That is it." Barnabas pushed open the conference room door. "Some of the guys are away at a conference that was planned months ago. A couple were needed at the work. That leaves just four of them here. Ladies, Bradon, Brennen, Brody, and Burnie, Abe are here. Emma sent more material for us."

Bradon was on his feet, reaching for the material, a measured look shared between Abe and himself. Bradon shook his head, knowing that Emma would have sent copies for them all. Ennis reached for some of the material, heading for the ladies, who had gathered at the far end of the room.

"What did Emma find, Abe?" Burnie stood beside him, his eyes on the documents.

"Not what we had hoped. I'll let you fellows work it. She's available if you need to speak with her. I have a meeting that I need to be at so I'm back on the road." He was gone before they could do more than call a thank you.

Brennen stared at the closing door before he turned to Barnabas.

"Did you know that he was coming?"

Barnabas shook his head.

"No, I didn't but it doesn't surprise me. Now, what do we have?"

"Names. Addresses. Connections." Burnie flipped through his papers. "These are interesting connections, I must say. Kat's been involved, I would hazard a guess."

"I'm sure that she has with her family tree program." Brody paused. "Now, this is interesting. It says that Oshea's parents are not who they seem to be."

Barnabas read over Brody's shoulder.

"That is interesting. I wonder if she knew that."

"Not likely, or she would have said something." Imly had approached. "I'm reading that her parents are involved in crime but Emma had questions about that."

"She does. We'll need to find Davy." Brennen looked around, ready to head for town.

"He's on the streets still, Brennen. Will can't get him to come in and work it from his desk."

"No, he won't. Not until he has all the information that he can find." Dallas had shown up, a frown appearing as he too glanced through the material. "Okay, fellows. The race is on. Let's see what we can find out."

"And that we will." Imly returned to the ladies, who had gathered closer, notepads and pens out, their conversation quiet.

Chapter 40

Coming in from being undercover, Davy was discouraged. He had tried, he thought, without success. His sources had tried as well, but there was just no word about Andy and Oshea. Does that mean that they're dead, he asked himself, or hidden away in another town? Somehow, he didn't think that. Davy turned as he heard his name, finding Branigan walking towards him.

"Davy? Any word?" Branigan was hoping and praying that there was.

"None." Davy peered around Branigan. "Simon, Lois, and Titus. Now, why doesn't that surprise me?"

Branigan gave a grin.

"They've been searching in their town to no avail. Titus said his sources on the street are silent."

"So they know nothing or are afraid to say." Davy and the four spoke for a few minutes before Branigan walked away.

"Davy, what can we do to help?" Simon worried about his young friends, even as he prayed for them.

"Right now? The only thing is to pray for them. We know God is in control of this situation. It's just hard."

Simon walked away at last, leaving Titus and Lois staring after him.

"He's hurting, Titus." Lois felt for her tender-hearted brother.

"He is. He became involved in something through no fault of his own. Now, we need to search. Only I have no idea where." Titus watched his wife, before he looked up to find Burnie and Blair standing there. "Fellows?"

"Branigan mentioned that you were in town and that he had spoken with you. Can you come to the building? Brody was looking for Simon. There just seems to be something about your town that is involved in all this." Blair felt that he was begging but didn't see any other option.

"Okay, we can do that. But where's Simon? We all came together." Titus turned to look for him, seeing Brody with him.

"Brody will bring him. If you'll follow us, let's head there."

Titus studied the whiteboards and then turned as Brendon approached him. He frowned for a moment as he watched the ladies working away, Lois with them.

"The ladies are here?" He was surprised.

"They are, Titus. At one point, we were in competition with them. This time? We're working together. We each look at this differently, research it differently, find things differently. In another day or so, we'll meet as a group and combine everything. We always find that our information overlaps but each piece that is different makes a whole. It's like a jigsaw puzzle."

"That it is. What's with the logic problem?" Titus was puzzled at that.

"Burnie, our author, set it up for one of the guys. We have just continued to use it. It helps us put everything we have confirmed into one spot, in a concise manner. Its scope will change as we work."

"I can see that. Now, what do you need from me? What can I tell you? Where can I help?"

"The thing that has puzzled us? It seems as if Oshea's kidnapper was headed for your town and had to be there at a certain time. Does that make sense?"

"Perfect sense. That's what struck me." Titus headed for a table and sat, pulling over a pad of paper and a pen. Brendon sat with him, watching closely. "So, if they had to be there at a certain time, that means that they were to meet someone. Only the storm moved in and Andy had to crash land. The kidnapper disappeared from the plane but showed up later. He had to have had help."

"That's what we think. And we think that where Andy landed? He would have been made to land close to there." Brendon pulled over topographical pictures and pointed. "This clearing? It's near where they went down. I talked to Ian, a friend and pilot, and emailed him the picture. He said that with the plane that Andy was flying, he could have landed there and taken off again."

"And who would they have had to pick up there? That's the million dollar question." Titus sat back, his eyes on Brendon. "You have thoughts about that."

"Just impressions. Oshea was taken for a reason. Andy was too. First as a pilot. But there's more to that than we know. We're hearing hints and rumours and finding bits and pieces." Brendon was frustrated.

"What you need is a computer program or data base to drop all this into. Do you have one?" Titus looked around as Jaxcy approached.

"We do now. Micah, a friend, has done that for us. He worked with his wife and his brother to set it up. He was through earlier today, Brendon, when you were out."

"That's good. Who's working it?"

"Berneen and Deri. Deri said she'll call in her brother and his wife if she needed to. His wife does computer work for the police department on an as needed basis."

"That's wonderful." Titus grinned at her. "Now to sort it all through and find out who it is." He frowned for a moment, his eyes on a lady working at a table near him. "That lady?"

"Who? Fynn?"

"Yes. What's she doing?" He was genuinely puzzled.

———

The pair with him began to laugh, causing him to frown deeper.

"That's Fynn. She's an entomologist and used to work for a medical examiner's office. She's working this like one of her cases, treating us all like her creepy crawlies."

"I most certainly am not." Fynn frowned before she began to laugh. "You are so right, Jaxcy. That's exactly what I'm doing. And I think I have found something that I need to research. I'll be back." Fynn was up and away before anyone could say anything.

"Did she just do that?" Titus stared in awe at the door.

"That's Fynn. Nothing stands in her way when she's on a mission. And she graduated with her master's degree at age 20. That's how her brain works." Jaxcy was away as well, heading for Neasa, Muir, and Ker.

Chapter 41

Fynn ran for the building, her eyes huge at what she had discovered. All that way back to that, she asked herself. How did Andy get involved? He's not from that town. But Oshea and Odell are.

She flew through the door to the conference room, bringing the men there to their feet. Brady was beside her, hugging her to stop in her tracks.

"Sweetheart? You flew in here. Someone chasing you?" He glared at the door, ready to charge through it and find whoever it was that had threatened his wife.

"No. Oh, no. It's not that." Fynn hugged him back. "I just discovered something, and I think it has a bearing on what we are looking at."

"Okay. So, can you share?" Brady was in awe of how Fynn's mind worked. She was always so far ahead of everyone else in her thought processes.

"I can." She was out of his arms, heading for a clear board and reaching for markers.

Cadee was there, her hand out for the markers.

"You talk. I write. Someone can tape what you're saying because I just know we'll have to go back over it again and again. That's what we always have to do with you, Fynn, just so that we can follow your thoughts."

Fynn grinned at her friend.

"Okay. So I spoke with Emma for a bit and then Kat. And I spoke with Darcy as well. She had called. She's sending a profile over to Brennen, she said."

"She is? Okay, let me see." Brennen opened his email. "And I have it. She asked that we not go to Davy. She wanted to do that."

"And she will." Fynn turned to the room, searching. "Buckley? Can we pray? I am praying that this helps, only I don't know that it will."

"We can certainly do that." Buckley's prayer was powerful, seeking protection for their friends, wisdom for the investigators, and a resolution to this adventure as he termed it. The other men followed after him, Breck finishing their time of prayer.

"Okay, Fynn, what do you have?" Barnabas stood near her, arms folded across his chest, his eyes not wavering from her face.

"So, we know that Oshea was targeted. The why of that? We always think the worse. Ransom. Human trafficking. Revenge. She saw something or someone. I don't think it's that. What I think is that she was taken to make someone do something or hand over something. And I don't think it's her parents that were targeted."

"That's an interesting thought, Fynn." Breck thought through her words. "How did you come up with that?"

"It wasn't clear for a long time. I was at my building, researching when a thought hit. We know that somehow or other her parents are likely involved. There has to be a link to Andy or his parents. I found a link. God help me, I didn't want to but I did." She pulled out a crumpled piece of paper from her pocket, opened it and stared at it. "Their parents are the link. From way back, when they were in college or university. They were all members of the same church, a smaller church. Did we ever discover that?"

The men stared at one another before they shook their heads.

"I'm not sure that we got back that far." Brennen was frustrated. "And we should have."

"We've been doing the best that we can, having to work, and not having a lot of information to go by." Blair spoke up, his eyes on Fynn. "Fynn, what else? How does it connect to Titus' town?"

"That I will come to. First, the parents. I haven't spoken with anyone yet. I'm leaving that to Davy and whoever it is that needs to do that. Dallas?"

Dallas nodded. "You're correct to do that, Fynn. We'll let Davy reach out to them and their town force. And your force as well, I think, Titus."

"No, it's okay. I'm working that investigation so I can take what you give me, verify it and go from there." Titus sat back, his eyes on Fynn. "Fynn?"

Fynn looked up, blinking for a moment as she came back to the room. Her face had paled even more than it had been.

"I have a horrible feeling, people. We need to find them and soon." She stared back at the boards, shooting out her words and details and facts, almost too fast for Cadee to write.

Imly shared a look with Guenivere, who nodded, holding up her phone. She knew that they always had trouble following Fynn and her thoughts, her words sometimes coming quicker than they could catch.

"Okay. So, we're in Titus' town. Who is related to the kidnapper? Who are his friends there?" Brody reached for his paperwork, handing part of it to Bradon.

"Here. These are listed as his friends. Here, in Oshea's town, and in Titus' town. Did we not connect them before?"

"I think that we had just done that this morning, Bradon." Brandon looked over shoulder, before he pointed to a name. "We came up with that one and Brennen searched the newspapers and found these other ones."

Titus had risen, and was reading over Bradon's shoulder as well. He drew a deep breath. He had a good idea of who was involved, but not why.

"I think I know who it is." All eyes were on Titus, Davy's included as he slipped through the door and then stood beside Breck, watching Titus closely. "He tries to keep out of the news and out of public eyesight, but the rumours have always been there that he is related to a criminal family and that they are trying to muscle there away into these towns."

Chapter 42

Davy turned at last, heading for the door, a pile of folders in his hands. It never failed to amaze him how the men and ladies here could find the information that they did. Emma had been in touch, just advising him that someone from Abe's security team was on his way with more information that she didn't feel she could send electronically. Where would they find him?

Barnabas approached him, holding the door open and then walking with him towards the building lobby. He was distressed, he knew, and had to pray hard. Bruce had been there earlier that morning and then headed out for a meeting he couldn't avoid.

"Barnabas? How do they do it? Dallas I get how he does. He told me over and over how these guys work but it's something to actually see in person." Davy stared through the windows towards the parking lot.

"I don't know, Davy, other than it's God. They seem to be able to find information, photos, documents, whatever it is that we need. They can't explain it other than God is the one doing it." Barnabas shrugged. "I have to agree. I've been there, doing that."

"I know. It helps but it also increases our workload. We have to look at what they found and how it fits in." Davy looked towards the parking lot once more as a truck pulled in and three men dropped down to the ground. "Do you know these men?"

Barnabas squinted and then grinned and nodded.

"I do. Some of Abe's security team. Ian. Micah. Joseph. This is good. He's sent the ones that we need. Ian is a paralegal but also his pilot. Micah is his computer expert. His wife is Kat who has sent on material. And Joseph does his security systems." He reached out a hand to shake those of the other men. "Welcome, fellows. Emma said you were on your way."

"We're here, Barnabas. Abe sent us and instructed us to help. Davy? You're here." Ian turned to him.

"I am and was just leaving. Something that you needed me for?" He searched the men's faces before he nodded. They know something and that's why they're here. "I have to head back to town. Come find me later today." He walked away, knowing that he wanted to stay but had other obligations.

"He's hurting, Barnabas, just because he can't find them."

"I know. All of us are." Barnabas stared into the distance. "What have you found?"

"We need to talk before we talk with the others." Micah hesitated. "Emma has found out what building that they were in. The rest of our team is heading that way. Abe wants us to stay with you all and work through what we have found and what you have found."

Barnabas' head shot around and he stared at Micah.

"You've found them? You know where they are?"

Ian nodded. "We have and we do. Abe's working through his plans right now and is in contact with the police force in that town. It's not here. It's not Oshea's town."

"Titus' town. That's what you're not saying. How do we tell him?" Barnabas shared a look with Breck who had come to stand beside him.

"It is. And we can't tell him. Not yet. Abe wants it kept as quiet as he can for now." Joseph nodded as Breck studied him. "He's not involved, but we know that there are officers who are. How many? That we are working through."

"When?" Aubrey's soft voice had the men turning her way.

"I'm sorry?" Micah looked at Barnabas. "I'm not sure what you mean."

"When did you find them?" Barnabas wrapped an arm around Aubrey as she stood there. She had come looking for him when he didn't return.

"Last night, just before midnight. Emma found the address earlier in the evening and she and Jace worked to confirm it. She has also confirmed the owner."

Aubrey muttered a name, bringing a nod from Micah.

"We found him too. Actually Fynn had. She has a list of names that some of the guys are working through."

"She has? That helps. How did she do that?" Joseph waved his hands, knowing Fynn. "Never mind. I don't know that we would follow her thought processes. She and Emma make a team on that."

Ian and Micah began to laugh at that, turning for the building.

"That they do." Joseph hesitated to follow, his eyes on the building and the surrounding area. Something was off, he thought, and began a systematic search, Breck watching and then joining him.

"Joseph? What are we searching for?" Breck stood upright for a moment, a hand rubbing at his face.

"That I'm not sure of." Joseph paused and then pointed. "Something just like that." He pointed to a metal box. "I don't think that belongs here."

Breck sighed, his phone out to call Davy back to the building. Joseph's team had discussed something like this, not knowing if the building family had received anything.

Breck stood at the building door an hour later, watching as the crime scene techs and the patrol

———

officers searched. Davy stood beside him, frustration evident.

"How long has it been here, Breck? Don't you search?" His words had a bite to them, not directed at Breck but at the situation.

"We do. I spoke with the security guards. They searched this morning, like always. Three times a day they do a thorough search just as Joseph did. It was not here earlier." Breck was frustrated and showed it, something not usual for him. But, he felt, they had been through enough. Too many of their friends had faced life and death situations.

Chapter 43

Davy stared down into the box, something that he felt he had done too many times. He was getting weary, he thought. Lord, I have no idea where our friends are. You do. You have the in the hollow of Your hand. I just don't understand man's depravity at times. And this is one of those times.

"That was all that was in it? No threats. No letters. No pictures. Just this?" Davy shook his head.

"That's all, Davy. An airplane pin. A lady's ring. Do they belong to Andy and Oshea?" Wendy, the tech, was puzzled as well. This was not making sense.

"I don't know. I don't recognize the ring." Davy stared at the building that he was standing beside. "I don't remember Oshea wearing one other than her wedding band and the engagement ring."

"And these are neither." Wendy frowned once more. "I'll log them into evidence, Davy. And see what happened." She walked away.

Davy turned, finding the men of the building and Titus standing nearby. Abe's three men stood further back, their gaze not on the men but on the surrounding area. Davy nodded. They watching for something or someone, aren't they, Lord? Doing what they do best.

"Davy?" Barnabas spoke for the group. He knew the ladies were in the lobby, watching. Simon stood with that group, his eyes intent on what was happening outside. Doc had been around and then walked away, rubbing at the back of his neck. He had an idea that he wanted to run with and Barnabas had simply nodded.

"Barnabas? Did Andy have an airplane pin that he wore?"

"No, he didn't. He only wore his watch and now his wedding band." Barnabas stared down at the photo Davy held in front of him. "I don't recognize either one of those. Oshea didn't wear jewelry. Aubrey commented that she was told Oshea didn't like jewelry."

"That's that then." Davy turned as he heard footsteps approaching. "Odell? You're here?"

"I am, Davy. Where are they?" He looked down at the photo. "That's Dad's airplane pin and Mom's ring. Where did they come from?"

"For the record, you recognize them, Odell? And identify them as belonging to your parents?"

"I do. Dad had flown when he was younger. Mom gave him that pin. And her ring? That's one her own parents had given her when she graduated from college. How did they end up here?" Odell was puzzled, that much was obvious.

"I don't know but I will find out. How be you go with Barnabas, Odell? Back into the building. I'll be in shortly." He watched as the men walked away, the building men following them before he approached Titus.

"Titus? Do you know their parents?"

"No, I don't think that I do. I don't recognize them at all. Why?" Titus' eyes were on the surrounding area.

"Because there seems to be a link to your town. That's where Andy was flying towards when he had to land. Now, you tell me why."

"I see. Let me look into that." Titus hesitated, knowing Davy wanted to say more and couldn't. "I know you can't say what all you're looking at. Talk to me or my chief. I have suspicions about a couple of officers. Just no proof."

"Let me have their names. I'll look into it as I can and without official notice, not unless I have to."

Titus nodded, giving the names. Davy kept his emotions off of his face, but the names were ones that he already had. What Titus had just said was confirmation in a way. He just had to provide the documentation to the town's chief and that would be done shortly.

Joseph approached Davy.

"That box? It was just put there today, Breck said."

"I know. There is nothing on the security cameras showing anyone coming in."

Joseph nodded. "I know. I've looked them over. Whoever it was either has an accomplice here or somehow managed to avoid the security system. And I would like to know how."

"So would I. Listen, I have to run again. I have another scene waiting for me. Keep me updated, please? I know that Abe's in town. He let me know that."

"He is, Davy, and I can't say why."

"I know that. Let me know what you can, when you can."

Ian and Micah moved to stand beside Joseph, supporting him in his search.

"Joseph, how did they do that? With the security here, they shouldn't have gotten through."

"I know. I have asked for the names of all the security people, the cleaners, the maintenance guys, the lawn care team. Emma and Jace will run them. Somewhere, there's a leak, once more."

Chapter 44

Moving quietly, Abe and the four of his team that he had with him approached the abandoned derelict building on an abandoned derelict property. It was outside of Andy's town but not close enough that word would have reached to the police force there. Emma had been certain that Andy and Oshea were there. Abe had studied her and then nodded. Emma would have proof, he knew.

"Abe, are we sure? It's pretty rundown." Murphy stood beside him, eyes watchful.

"Emma was certain. Let's prove her right once again." Abe turned, eying Nathaniel, Matt, and Luke. "Prayers first fellows and then we move in." His eyes raised to Doug Foster, his cousin, but also the lead for their town's ETF force, and another lifelong friend, Dave Allison, a paramedic. "We move in and move out as quickly as we can."

Nathaniel, the sniper on Abe's team, stood where he was under cover but could watch. The others moved in quietly, eyes alert. He turned as he heard a sound and then moved towards the man, no, youth, he thought who was approached. The youth jumped in

——

surprise and shock as Nathaniel appeared in front of him. Nathaniel's hand on his arm kept him from disappearing.

"This way. And don't say a word. I'll gag you if you do." Handcuffs clicked on the youth's wrists, who remained defiant. Nathaniel forced him to sit, in front of him, where he could watch him at the same time as he watched for his teammates and friends.

Abe peered through the duskiness in the building. It was still daylight but the building was dim. Dust and cobwebs were aplenty. Matt pointed to the rough floor. Footprints were in evident, multiple ones at that. They spread out, searching before a click on Abe's comlink had him turning and then heading for Doug.

"In here, Abe. There's a door that's hidden. It fits so well with the wall that we would not have seen it." Doug felt along the edge and found the hidden latch. His eyes met Abe's and then those of the other men.

"We're in first. Then Matt and Dave. You others watch closely. This is where the danger is, I suspect." Abe pulled open the door, a frown on his face as it didn't squeak or creak as he expected it to. "That's strange."

"Someone's oiled it." Matt followed, his weapon ready. "There. Over there. Another door? Where does it lead to?" He reached for it, pulling it open. "Stairs? What is this?"

"I have no idea. Lead on, Matt." Abe, Doug, and Dave followed him, leaving Luke and Murphy standing guard for them. "There. Another door. This is really strange, guys. Abe reached for the door this time, finding once more that it opened easily under his hand.

The men stood, looking around at the room. It had been dry walled and painted. This is so strange, Doug thought, before he looked around. A sound from Dave brought his attention that way as Dave sprang to kneel beside a lady.

"It's Oshea. She's in rough shape, Abe." Dave spun for a moment as he heard a sound from Matt and saw him on his knees beside Andy. "Matt?"

"He's alive as well, Dave. We can't do much for them here." With Doug's help, Matt had Andy up and over his shoulders, catching a glimpse of Oshea being gathered into Dave's arms.

The men moved rapidly, heading for Nathaniel and then their vehicles. Abe's steps slowed as he approached him, his eyes on the youth.

"Nathaniel? Who is this?"

"I have no idea. He was heading your way when I stopped him." He looked towards the vehicles. "How are they?"

"Unconscious. We'll know more once we get them seen to." Abe headed for his vehicle. "Nathaniel, I'll drop you and Murphy here with Doug. Talk to the authorities. And send them out here. They'll want to see this place."

Barnabas turned from where he had been studying the whiteboards. Stephen and Sarah stood beside him, despair on their face that they would ever see their son again. He pulled out his phone, squinting at the number before he moved away, turning to watch the activity in the room.

"Abe? You're calling. Tell me that you have news." Barnabas had hope but also fear.

"I just spoke with Davy. We're on our way to your town. Nathaniel, Murphy, and Doug are in Simon's town." Abe turned for a moment in his seat, his eyes on Andy, who had not roused at all.

"They are? Abe?" Barnabas shook his head at Breck, who had come to stand with him.

"We have them, Barnabas. We're heading for the hospital in your town. They're alive but unconscious. We're about thirty minutes out." Abe heard the sharply indrawn breath. "God helped us find them, Barnabas. He has them."

"I know. We were just so afraid that they were dead and buried somewhere that we would never find." Barnabas slowly pocketed his phone and looked up. Bruce stood beside him, a hand on his shoulder, Breck on his other side.

"Son? You have news?" Bruce saw the hope and determination on Barnabas' face.

"Abe found them. He's on his way in to the hospital with them. He hasn't said much but then he can't." He watched as Abe's men approached him. "Your team found them, Micah." He walked away, leaving the other men staring after him, heading for Buckley.

"Buckley? We need to pray." Barnabas groaned. "I'm sorry. I shouldn't have worded it that way. Andy and Oshea are safe."

Buckley's face lit up. "They are. Okay. People? Let's pray. I'm told that Andy and Oshea are safe. We pray, we search, and we send in a team to where they are."

There were cheers from the men and tears from the ladies as they gathered in a circle to pray and then to sort out who would go and who would stay. They all wanted to go but knew that they couldn't.

Chapter 45

Stephen and Sarah almost ran into the Emergency Department, desperate to find their son and his bride. This shouldn't have happened, they thought. Who was that desperate to harm them? Bradon had approached them about knowing Oshea's parents in college. They had looked at one another, and then Stephen had frowned.

"I can vaguely remember a couple by that name, but I'm not sure that we ever met them. We went to the same church, but they never got involved. Not that we did much either." He stared at the floor. "Did we do something that we shouldn't have back then? Is this why that happened to Andy and Oshea?"

"We don't know that. It's all speculation at the moment. It was just a question that we had." Bradon had moved on, leaving them looking at one another.

Sarah drew a deep shuddering breath as she sat, her hand in her husband.

"Do you really think it goes back that far?"

"It might. The boys will research it as I know they are. I can't see it but it's possible, I guess."

Doc looked around as Barnabas approached him as he stood outside for a moment, catching a breath of fresh air and some sunshine before it turned to dark. It had been a busy day and he was tired.

"Barnabas? Which one of the fellows are you here for?"

"Doc, Abe and his men went in. Andy and Oshea are on their way."

"They found them? Praise the Lord!" Doc turned, pulling Barnabas with him. "Did they say much?"

"Other than they were unconscious, no. It will be a police investigation now." Barnabas stopped at the ambulance bay, watching as Andy and Oshea were lifted to stretchers and then pushed into the department. "Come find us when you can. Stephen and Sarah are here."

"As I expected they would be. Oshea's people?" Doc disappeared before Barnabas could say a word.

Abe approached him, his walk slow, not quite sure how to tell Barnabas what they had found. He knew that he had to be careful what he said, that he couldn't say a lot.

"Abe? What can you tell me?" Barnabas pointed towards where Breck was waiting.

"Not a lot, you know that, Barnabas. We had an address for an abandoned place. I spoke with the police there and they said we could go in and search, seeing it was abandoned. We went in and found them.

I can't give the details, as you know. But we did find a youth heading for them, and Nathaniel stopped him."

"A youth? That's bizarre." Breck was puzzled for a moment.

"Not really, Breck. He was sent in, he did tell us, just to monitor them." Abe looked towards the hospital. "We need to run. Doug and Dave are on duty in the morning and we have a team in for training. Glad we could help once more, Barnabas. Call if we can do anything else." With that, Abe ran for his vehicle and they headed away.

"This is strange, you know, my friend. And a youth involved?" Breck looked around Barnabas to see Davy approaching. "And here's Davy. And Will."

Davy stood, his head tilted back and eyes closed as he drew in a deep breath. Will remained silent, not sure what all the building men had been told. He was there as a friend at that point in time, not the police chief.

"Davy? What can you tell us or is it too soon?"

"It's too soon. I'm just glad that they're back with us. I'll need to speak with them before you fellows and ladies do." He walked away, heading for the couple and the physicians treating them.

"Will?" Breck looked over at him, seeing the peace on his face, and prayed for that for them all.

"Here as a friend tonight, Breck. Now, let's head in and find Stephen and Sarah. I have word that the police in her town are reaching out to Oshea's parents."

Breck's steps paused for a moment before he spoke.

"You know, it's strange that her parents have never come around. Do you know why?"

Will nodded. "I do, and it's part of the investigation. Not a happy part, I must say."

Chapter 46

Andy slowly roused, puzzled to find himself in a bed with blankets covering him. He was warm, he decided, before he looked around. His eyes closed again and he slept. Sarah watched, concern on her face, even as Stephen's arm came around her.

"He was awake?" Stephen's voice was low.

"Just for a moment. I don't think he roused enough to know where he is."

"Not likely. Come on, love. We're needing to leave. We'll be back in the morning." He led her from the room and to where Oshea lay, still unconscious, battered and bruised to some extent.

"Oshea hasn't awakened yet." Sarah was worried about the younger woman. "What did they do to her?"

"She may have given up, Sarah." His hand reached to gently touch Oshea's hair. "We'll leave her with God, love. I just wonder where her parents are." Stephen led Sarah away and down the hall, finding Bradon and Benen waiting for them. "And here are two of the boys."

"Waiting for us?" Sarah reached to hug them, considering them close friends.

"We are. We'll escort you home, unless you want to go back to the building."

Stephen and Sarah shared a look.

"How about the building, Benen? I want to see where you are all at with your research. I know that you haven't packed it in and gone home to your families."

"Some of us have. We're working in shifts, Stephen, just so we don't burn out."

"And that's a possibility." Sarah settled down in the car, her eyes on the night sky. "God is in control, boys. Even when it doesn't seem like He is, He is. We don't know what His plans are for this, why He has allowed it, why they were gone so long. We have no idea of what they were put through and they may never tell us." She shared a look with Stephen. "It's hard on us not knowing. That's where our faith comes in. Titus and Lois headed home as did Simon. But before they left, I had a really good and long talk with them. Titus has seen much on the job that has affected him and that he can't share. The same for Simon. Lois has been their prayer warrior, supporting both of them. I am not sure if you are aware, but Simon lost his fiancée just as they were to marry. An unforeseen medical condition took her and quickly. He remained true to her. That's what love is." She paused. "I can see that love with Andy and Oshea. They will need our support and love to get through this. And they will. But they'll never be the person that they were before. You both know that only too well."

Bradon and Benen shared a look and nodded. She was right. Their adventures, as they were termed, had changed them. They found that they didn't trust strangers quite as readily and worried about their wives and the children that were in their homes. They knew that every member of their building family was the same. They would support Andy, speak with him, find him the resources that he needed. The ladies would do that for Oshea.

Andy roused again during the early morning hours, rubbing at his eyes. He squinted in the low light before he shoved at the blankets. He was on his feet, finding his clothes and dressing rapidly, or as rapidly as he could. That he was in a hospital? They must have been found, he thought. But he needed to find Oshea. She had been threatened so much. Andy had no idea where she was, if she was in the same hospital, or in a funeral home. His heart dropped at that last thought. *Please, Lord, don't let me lose her. That's what they threatened. I can't lose the love of my life, not yet.* Then, Andy sighed. *I'm sorry, Lord. Here I am telling You what to do. It's Your will, not mine. That I know.*

Andy walked quietly through the hallways, not seeing the nurse watching him. He paused, looking around, not sure where to go.

"Andy?" The nurse's voice was quiet as she stood near him. "The room to your right. That's where Oshea is."

He stared at her, not sure that he had heard correctly.

"She's here? She's still alive? I thought that she was dead." Tears momentarily blinded him.

Her hand on his back, the nurse turned him to the room door.

"Go on in, Andy. No one will say anything. She hasn't roused yet, but we didn't think that she would. It's enough that you are on your feet. Just don't overdo it." She watched as Andy shuffled as he walked towards his bride before she turned, heading for the desk to document that Andy was up.

His hand on the side rail of the bed, Andy stared down at Oshea, not seeing the marks, the bruising, her pallor, the dark circles under her eyes. He saw instead his beautiful beloved wife. Tears blinded him before he angrily wiped at them. Weeping didn't help, he thought, not realizing that tears indeed would help him heal. His hand reached for hers, finding her fingers curling around his.

Oshea gave a soft sigh and turned her face, knowing in her unconscious state, that Andy was near her, not like it had been for so many days. Andy had been kept away from her, not allowed to approach her or touch her. Their captor had seen to that.

Andy's head raised as he stared at the equipment before he looked for a chair. He pulled in over as close to the bed as he could get, not willing to have any distance between them. He wrapped himself in a blanket he found as well, unable to get past the chill that seemed to sink bone deep.

<hr>

Buckley stood in the doorway, having felt compelled to return. Locklin was with him, her heart rising in prayer for their friends.

"Buckley? Andy's up. I didn't think that he would be."

Shaking his head, Buckley moved towards Andy, startling the other man who spun on his chair, fear on his face.

"Buckley? You're here? It's the middle of the night."

Buckley simply grinned at Andy.

"I am. God gave me orders to be here and I couldn't refuse. How are you?"

"Sore, disoriented, angry." Andy bit out his words, his eyes back on Oshea. "And wanting Oshea to awaken. They were rough on her."

"We can see that." Locklin simply hugged him and then moved to stand near the bed. "Have they said anything to you yet?"

"Not that I know of. I just woke up a while ago and found Oshea." Andy drew in a deep breath. "And I have to talk to Davy and soon. There's a timeline that we were given. Only I don't know how we were to reach it when we were kept locked up. Do you?"

Chapter 47

Wrapped in a blanket, a pair of Andy's heavy socks on her feet, Oshea curled up in the corner of their couch. Andy watched her closely, not wanting to smother her but needing to be with her. He handed her a hot drink and then sank down beside her, weary beyond what he had ever expected to be or experienced. His head went back on the couch as his eyes slid closed.

Oshea shifted enough to watch him, worry in her heart for him. Andy had been threatened as had her family. She didn't understand why, though. Their abductor had not been clear. And she could give no real description of him. He had ensured that.

"Andy? What do we do?" Oshea's voice was hesitant, a sign that she was unsure of herself.

"Oshea? About what they asked of us?" Andy turned his head without raising his, puzzlement on his face.

"That. And us? How do we stay safe? I know that Davy has someone outside the door for now. Was it only two days ago that we were rescued?" Oshea's eyes slid shut as a tear trickled down her cheek. Her hand raised to wipe it away, feeling Andy just sweeping her into his arms.

"I have no idea, sweetheart. That's the problem, isn't it? I'm not sure that we can. Davy had people search our home and outside. Joseph has been around, setting up stronger security for us. But we will be out and about, on our own. We can't have someone with us all the time."

"I know. It's just that I don't know what they were asking, do you?" Oshea turned to him, finding his eyes on her.

"No, it was strange. It was like it was a fishing expedition where they really didn't expect to find anything. Did you know him?"

Oshea shook her head, thinking back to their abductor. She frowned for a moment, lost in thought.

"No, I don't. Do you?"

Andy shook his head in turn.

"No, I haven't never seen him before. It's just so strange." Andy repeated his words, a frown covering his face. "And he really wasn't clear on what he wanted, was he?"

Oshea's head went down on Andy's shoulders as she drifted off to sleep. Andy held her, praying for his bride and for a quick resolution of whatever it was they faced. The couple had talked over the last couple of days since they returned home, finding all the verses in the Bible that they could for strength, for protection, for God's love for them, and His will for them as well.

———

They just didn't understand why they were going through what they were.

Andy's mind drifted back to that fateful day, to the day when they were taken from their home. Davy had been around and they had spoken with him about it. He had asked questions that they could not or would not answer. He had risen to his feet, sternly telling them that if they remembered anything, he needed to know, sooner rather than later.

Andy and Oshea had risen early that morning, knowing his parents would be there shortly after breakfast. They had had no real plans, just wanting to spend time together. Oshea has laughed as Andy had shrugged when she asked him what his plans actually were.

Finishing their breakfast and cleaning up their mess, Oshea had opened the back door, intending on wandering the yard. Andy and she had talked about what they were wanting to change and she had had an idea she wanted to see if it would work. A scream had risen from her as she stared at the man standing in the doorway, his hand on the door to prevent Oshea from slamming it closed.

Andy had slid to a halt as he ran for her, his hands raising in the air as a weapon was pointed at him. His eyes had shifted between the man and Oshea, suddenly feeling someone behind him and he was pushed forward, barely keeping to his feet. He had reached for Oshea's hand, feeling hers trembling with the fear, no terror, that she felt.

Forced from their house, the door closed behind them, they had been walked to the street and then down it to a waiting van. Oshea was shoved in and to the rearmost seat, Andy to the middle seat. They were not given an opportunity to try and flee, a man sitting beside each one. Andy frowned as he stared at the driver, a woman. Now what, he asked himself? How do I get Oshea free without getting her hurt?

Driving around town for a while, the driver headed at last for the highway and accelerated. She nodded at the low command from the man sitting beside her. She knew where he wanted to head. She just didn't like it. She had signed on as his driver, not knowing that she would be part of a kidnapping. And that was exactly what it was.

Pulling to a stop near the decrepit building, she turned off the motor and waited. This was what she always did. He was specific in his orders and waiting for him to decide what he wanted to do was one of them.

The man shifted in his seat, watching the young couple. He smiled with glee as he saw the fear on Oshea's face and then frowned at the determination and lack of fear on Andy's. They would soon take them from him, he thought.

Forced into the building, Andy and Oshea were kept separate, the men between them. They exchanged puzzled glances as they stared around. A frown covered Andy's face as the secret door was opened and they were shoved through into the next room. Another door opened and they were shoved down the stairs, barely able to keep to their feet. Separated in the room,

Andy kept his eyes on Oshea, who shrank back as the man approached her, a hand out to touch her hair.

Andy gave a yell and charged at the man, his surprise move taking the man to the floor. Andy's arms were gripped in a tight manner, the pain from that not noticed, as he was pulled off the man and then slammed against a wall, his arms held out from his sides. He was unable to escape, no matter how he struggled. His yells to leave Oshea alone echoed through the room.

The man rose, brushing off his expensive suit, a hateful and vengeful look on his face. He turned to Oshea, finding her huddled in fear against the opposite wall to Andy.

"You will both pay for that move, little lady. You will never leave this room." He studied his nails before he brought out a syringe and then approached her, his hand catching her arm before she was jabbed with the needle. She sank to the floor, her eyes closed, not hearing Andy's roars to leave her alone.

The man then turned to Andy and repeated the move, not watching as Andy fought him and then sank to the floor as well. He turned to the men and nodded, walking away, leaving the men to follow.

Andy and Oshea lay where they had fallen, not hearing the door click closed behind the men, the lights left on in their underground dungeon. They little knew what fate awaited them over the next weeks.

———

Chapter 48

How much later it was when he roused, Andy never knew. He sat up, his head spinning and his stomach roiling from the sedation that he had been given. Blinking his eyes to try and clear them, he stared around, his gaze finding Oshea.

"Oshea?" He was across the room, on his knees beside her, trying to rouse her and not succeeding. "What did they do to us?" He sat back, Oshea in his arms, as he looked around. No windows? And only the outline of a door. Off to the side he could see a rudimentary washroom. *Someone planned and prepared this,* he thought. *Are we the first to be here? Or have others been here and died here? Lord, I am scared. Scared that we won't make it out. Scared that I will die and that Oshea will suffer, for what reason we have no idea.*

They were left alone for the first day or so. Oshea had roused, finding food and water on a table in the corner. They were unsure if they should eat but felt that they had to. She searched the room, desperate to find a way out. Only there was no way. The door didn't open.

"This is strange, Andy. Who does this?" She had come to a standstill in the centre of the room, her arms wrapped around herself.

Andy had been leaning against a wall, trying to come up with a plan and failing.

"I don't know, sweetheart. I wish I did. Did you recognize him at all?"

Oshea shook her head, turning to face him.

"I didn't. Did you?"

Andy shook his head in turn before he walked towards her and simply wrapped her in his arms.

"No, I didn't, but he seemed to know us. And I would like to know why."

They slept, wrapped in each other's arms, not hearing the door open. A rough shove with a booted foot roused Andy and then Oshea. They scrambled to their feet, their hands held with one another, as they faced the monster as Oshea termed him.

"What do you want?" Andy went on the offensive, wanting to find out why and then to find a way out.

"Not happening, boy." The man turned his cruel look towards Oshea. "She's going to cooperate with me."

"I don't know you. Why would I do that?" Oshea touched her lip, wiping away the blood that had happened as she was backhanded across the face. She could hear Andy's struggles and yells for her to be left alone.

"You will cooperate, young lady. This is only a taste of what you will receive if you don't. I will be back and you will talk with me."

He walked away, leaving Andy to reach for Oshea.

"Are you okay?" His finger gently touched her lip.

"I am, Andy. And you?" At his nod, she frowned. "What does he want? I don't know him. Have nothing that isn't mine."

This same scene repeated itself for days. He would ask Oshea to cooperate, her statement being that she didn't know what he wanted. Andy was always held against the wall despite his struggles to escape.

The last day came, the man appearing mid-morning. He stared at Oshea and then Andy before he pointed at Andy. One of the men pulled out a syringe and used it on him, despite his struggles. Oshea watched horrified as Andy slumped to the floor, unconscious, she prayed and not dead.

"This is what happens, little lady. You have not cooperated with us. He dies. And you do too."

"But I don't know you. I don't know what you want. Can't you tell me?" She stared at him in horror as he finally did, not feeling the hands on her arm or the prick of a needle. Her head was shaking as she too lost consciousness and dropped to the floor.

The man watched them without any compassion and then walked away. It mattered little to him that they would die there. He would send in the youth that he had found to make sure that they were still there. A few days after that? He would send in his men to recover their bodies and bury them somewhere they would never be found. He would move on to his next target, Andy's parents.

Chapter 49

Andy roused slightly a few hours later but not enough to fully focus on where he was or what had happened. He dropped back into the well of unconsciousness, not aware that they had been left to die. Oshea never moved from where she lay, her unspoken despair driving her to give up and prepare herself to die and never be found.

Hours later, the door opened carefully, and men entered. These men were here to help them, not bring further distress to them. Abe watched as Matt and Dave assessed the pair and then gathered them up to head for the stairs and freedom.

They were not aware of the efforts taken on their behalf to rouse them in the vehicles, or the efforts by Doc and the emergency room staff. They were still in that darkness, a darkness that sometimes precludes death. That was what they had determined would happen, and they were prepared for it.

Oshea had roused early that next morning, her eyes blinking as she focused. A soft sound came from her as she realized that she was free. She shoved at the blankets, finding her one hand caught in another's.

She turned her head, a softening coming to her face as she watched Andy sleep, uncomfortable as his position was in the chair. *We are both free,* Oshea thought. *But how and who? And just where is that man?* She slept, not hearing the nurse moving around her room.

Davy stood later that morning, but still early, his eyes shifting between the two. He had the statements that they had given, but still had questions.

"You don't know that man, that's correct?" His voice was neutral, not giving away what he was thinking.

"That's correct. I have never seen him." Oshea's brow wrinkled for a moment. "Why me? Do you know why, Davy?"

Davy shook his head.

"We don't, Oshea. And we have what description that you both have given. Unfortunately, we can't find him. There is a youth in custody with that town's force but he's not saying much."

"Where were we?" Andy was puzzled, that much he admitted to himself.

"Near Simon's town. That's where you were being directed that day, Andy, the day that you had your plane crash. We have evidence that this room was prepared at that point. As to why? That we're getting a clearer picture of but we don't have a definite reason yet."

"And if you don't, then how do we stay safe?" Oshea refused to look at him.

"Don't put yourselves out there. He'll take you again. The next time? You won't come home. Do you really want to put your families and friends through that?" Davy walked away, frustration evident on his face, before he had a thought and pulled out his phone, sending off a quick text message to Titus and then to Barnabas.

They had gone home that afternoon, fearful that they would disappear again, fearful that someone would break into their home, but glad to be at home. Their trust in God had been shaken by the events but they were determined not to let anything stop them.

Breck and Bradon had stared at them later that day, shaking their heads at their adventure.

"And it was a room set up just for you, do you think?" Breck was thinking through what had been said.

"I would suspect so." Andy rubbed at his cheek. "It was dry walled, painted, had a rudimentary washroom. It was just so strange. A prison nonetheless."

"And he kept asking you about a man, a name, an event?" Bradon shook his head at that. "Without giving any details?"

"That's right. I don't understand that, Bradon. And why me? What did I ever do to him?" Oshea was angry but also puzzled at that.

"I don't think that you did anything. Nor did Andy. We have determined that both sets of your parents were in the same church when at college or university. They didn't know each other than by name, Andy. We spoke with your parents about that. So we are tracing who they might have known then. It's a long process."

"I could see that it would be. Did Dad give any sense of what he might know?"

Breck shook his head.

"He's puzzled as well. He stated that he has no idea why this has happened. And we believe him. Your mom as well is adamant that she had never met Oshea's parents. Odell knew nothing about this."

"Odell? Of course he does. He went back to that town and church just a week or so ago." Oshea shook her head. "I have no idea why. Have you asked him?"

"Unfortunately, we can't do that. He's disappeared. And so have your parents, Oshea. The police are searching for them, only they have no idea where to look." Breck was frustrated.

Oshea stared at him and then turned to Andy, a thoughtful look on her face.

"Have you searched for all their properties?"

"They have more than one?" Bradon stared at her. "We know about your home."

"They have a couple of others. Not in their name. The names they used? I don't know who they are but these are them." She quickly reached for paper and pen, scrawled down the names, and handed it to him. "One is a cottage on the shore of Lake Erie. The other is near the Quebec border."

"I see." Breck reached for the paper. "And these are the names they are under? I don't remember seeing them when we searched."

"No, they had hidden these properties. And now I have to wonder why. What did they want to hide?" Oshea rose and walked away, Andy standing and watching her.

"Andy?" Breck's voice reached through his thoughts to bring Andy's head around to study him.

"Breck? Can you look into those before you pass them on to Davy? And ask Emma too, if you would."

"We will do that, but Davy does need to know at some point."

Andy sighed, watching Oshea as she stood in the hallway. "We know he does. Just look into them for me? And Oshea? I would rather hear from you what you find and so would Oshea."

Breck nodded before he prayed for the younger couple, walking away with Bradon.

"Breck? This is bizarre. Why the different names?"

"It sounds as if they're on the run from something or are involved in something. I pray that it's because they are on the run." Breck pulled away from the curb, not seeing any vehicle that stood out to him as watching Andy's place. "They'll need some help, those two."

"We are praying for them but you're right. They will need help." Bradon scrolled through his phone, sending off a text message. "I contacted Darby and not likely should have. She's been that concerned about them."

"She'll be good for them to talk with. She's helped others of us."

Chapter 50

Three days later, Oshea's hand tight in his, Andy paused outside of the conference room door. They had been asked to come, that there was material they needed to see. His parents were there as well.

Andy stared down at Oshea before he bent to kiss her. Her head went against him for a moment.

"No matter what they have found, Oshea, just now that I love you deeply. I can't see my life with anyone else but you. God brought us together, even how it happened."

Oshea nodded, her thoughts muddled for a moment.

"I love you too, Andy. I just wish it could have been different, how we met. This is draining, what we have been through. It affects us and it affects those around us." She looked up. "Do you think that we would have met otherwise?"

Andy shrugged, biting at his lip, a new habit that he had picked up.

"I would like to think so. God meant for us to be together, that I have no doubt of. And He would have done just that, you know."

"I know." Oshea stared at the closed door. "Do we really want to go in there?"

Andy gave a small laugh.

"We may not want to, but we do have to. As much as I would like to run away with you and find somewhere safe to live, they have been working this for us. They must have some sort of answer to ask us to be here."

"I hope you're right." Oshea pushed open the door, Andy following her through it, to stand and stare at the activity going on. "They have made progress, Andy." She walked towards the whiteboards, Ennis and Imly approaching her, the other ladies gathering around her. Sarah reached to hug her, keeping an arm around Oshea.

"Andy?" Brennen stood beside him, Dallas on his other side. "How are you two?"

Andy shrugged before he spoke, wishing it was different.

"About how you two were at this point. Tell me. Have you solved it?"

Brennen nodded.

"We think we have. There is enough that we can turn it over to Davy today. Emma and Abe are on their way and should be here. They wanted to speak with you two about this."

Andy sagged for a moment with relief, his eyes on Stephen as he stood in front of his son.

"Dad?"

"They tell me they have the answers, son. It's only a matter of Davy verifying what they have given him and doing his own investigation on it. Davy tells me that he is almost to the point of making arrests. The youth that Nathaniel stopped has been talking." Stephen frowned for a moment. "He is just sixteen. He had no idea what he was walking into that day. We need to work with him and find him help."

"It's already done, Stephen." Blair stood beside the older man. "We've reached out and put him in touch with people that will help."

"Thank you. That is what this Foundation does, isn't it? Be encouragers to others." He turned, watching Oshea. "Andy, how is Oshea?"

"Hurting, Dad. Uncertain. Not ready to hear the answers but knowing that she has to." He turned slightly. "Breck, we're ready to do that?"

"We are, Andy, but first we spend time in prayer, particularly for you and Oshea and both sets of parents." Breck walked towards Buckley, who nodded and then spoke over the noise in the room, drawing attention to himself as he asked them to sit and spend time in prayer.

Chapter 51

With his arm around Oshea, Andy raised his head, searching for answers on the faces of his friends. He nodded. *This is it, isn't it, Lord? Today we find out why.* He heard the sound of the door softly closing and looked to see Davy and Will finding seats. Andy frowned as to why they were there.

Breck looked up from where he and Barnabas had been sitting, their heads close together as they spoke. He nodded at Will, knowing that the two were there as friends more than as officers.

Breck stood, heading for the whiteboards and reaching for a marker.

"Okay. Andy and Oshea? We have answers for you, finally. This is what we have discovered, between ourselves and Emma and Kat. I don't know how those two ladies do it, but they have come through once more.

"Andy and Oshea, your parents were in the same church. We talked about that. Both have said that they never met the other, knew the names but it went no further. We'll come back to that.

"Stephen and Sarah, you settled here, Sarah's hometown. Stephen, you opened up your photography business and it has grown. Sarah, you have worked with him as much as you can.

"Oshea, your parents went into business, a financial one. Odell worked in the IT department and you did not work for them in any department. We can reassure you that their businesses are legitimate. There is no criminal activity involved in any of them. Bruce and Blair have talked at length with them. They were horrified to hear what had happened with you. They had received threats against themselves and fled to one of their properties, thinking to keep you and Odell safe. The reason for the names? They were inherited properties and the stipulation was that the names could not be changed for a number of years. That time frame has just passed.

"Odell had been investigating something to do with the threats, not realizing how much danger that he was in. That's why he has been acting like he has been. The same for your parents.

"Now, as to why. That took some work. We've had to dive deeply into the past of your parents and your grandparents. None are or were involved in criminal activities. That we can reassure you of. Blair has more information that I will let him explain."

"Thanks, Breck." Blair retrieved a marker, approached the whiteboard and wrote down one name before he turned, catching the nod that Stephen gave. "This is who is behind it all. Stephen, you know of him, we think?" They all caught Stephen's nod.

"Oshea? This man? Dudley Littlejohn? He knows your parents. In fact, we have evidence that he has been tracking them for years. His father was the minister of the church you went to, Stephen. Did you know him at all?"

Stephen shook his head as he glanced down at Sarah.

"No, I don't think we did. I mean, we knew the minister's name but that was all. The church was not real forthcoming with names, come to think of it."

"No, they weren't. They weren't real friendly. We had spoken of finding another church, but it was closest to us and the messages seemed all right." Sarah shook her head. "I don't remember him at all."

"But he remembered you. The word that we have received, now that Andy and Oshea are free, is that he bears a grudge of some kind against you four. That we are awaiting confirmation on. He has a brother who is not involved in crime, as he is. That brother has lived away from here for years. A passing word from a friend has brought him back. His name? He changed it. We know him as Thomas Browne."

"Tom Browne? The photographer?" Stephen shared a look with Sarah. "We know him, have spoken with him, but that's about it. Could he not have stopped this?"

Brendon spoke up.

"No, he wasn't aware of what his brother was doing. The name that he goes by is the name that he chose to do his photography under. Not many people are aware of his connection to this area."

"And Dudley has always had to take the teasing and the taunts for his first name. That is a big reason for driving him to crime and to what he has done." Bradon looked around at his friends. "This has driven him since he was young, well before he met you two. Why he decided that you four would be his victims, that is something that is really bizarre."

Stephen shared a look with Andy and Oshea, his hand tightening on his wife's.

"And that would be?"

"He wanted a friendship with you four, only you didn't acknowledge him. He didn't understand that you had never met him, that your interests and his would never make that possible."

"And so he chose to bring harm to Oshea and through her to Andy?" Sarah was dismayed and she could feel anger building inside her. "I still don't get why them."

"The same reason is what we're hearing. You four went on to build successful lives, with families. He could never do that. No woman would marry him, let alone date him. He would abusive from the first and that reputation preceded any overture he would make to date a lady." Brandon shook his head. "I have confirmation that he has killed a least one woman because she shunned him."

———

"This is so bizarre, Brandon. I really don't understand how his mind works." Andy was trying to work through what he had been told.

"I understand it, Brandon." Oshea turned to Andy. "You weren't close enough to see his face and in particular his eyes. His eyes are dead, as they say. There is no life in them. The only thing that keeps him going is what he can get away with in a criminal path. He left us to die because I wouldn't or couldn't give him what he wanted." Oshea had paled. "Lord, forgive me. I blocked it out."

Chapter 52

Andy's arms were around Oshea as she sobbed. Locklin moved in beside her, a hand on hers as she prayed for the other lady. Stephen and Sarah were on their feet, moving to stand behind their son and his wife, their hands on his.

"Oshea?" Barnabas had moved in, to crouch down in front of her, raising his eyes as he saw Davy standing beside him. "What did you forget?"

Oshea looked up and they all drew in a deep breath at the sad and haunted look on her face.

"He told me why me. Why I had been kidnapped. What he wanted from me." She bit at her lip, unable to continue for the sobs rising in her. "He has a son. He kidnapped the boy when he was young and raised him as his own. He told me that I was kidnapped to marry his son, that that would be his revenge on Mom and Dad. I didn't know about Andy when I was kidnapped. Apparently, he thought that if he made Andy part of the kidnapping, that Andy would be arrested and charged as well. He didn't know that we would crash land and that Andy and I were married. That's why he left us in that room. He wanted us to die and our families to never know where we were. He planned to bury us somewhere that no one would ever find us."

Andy's arm tightened around the love of his life, sorrow that she had to be told that and anger that she had been. There was also fear for her. He began to pray, to petition God to protect her.

The men were on their feet, heading for their work stations. Dallas crouched down in front of Oshea.

"Oshea? We'll need you to come in and add that to your statement. How does Odell fit in?"

"He doesn't. He didn't care about Odell. Just wanted me to pay and when I did to make Mom and Dad pay. Where are they?"

"We have them safe, Oshea. They want to see you very badly. They are sorry that they seemed distant over the last few months, just as you thought, but they had been receiving letters and threats directed at them. From Littlejohn we now know. They thought if they kept distant from you, that you would be safe. The silent partner that was mentioned? That was a red herring thrown at us by Littlejohn. There were no other relatives outside of the province. The statement that your parents were gone and that these were their friends raising you? Part of the plot to exact revenge. The man who assaulted me? An imposter, having had plastic surgery to look like your father."

"I need my Mom. Can she come?" Oshea turned to bury her head against Andy.

———

"We can do that." Will Peters had moved away, his phone out to contact the police chief in Oshea's town.

"Andy, I need air. Is it safe to go outside?" Oshea was on her feet, running from the room and then from the building, Andy following her.

Bradon and Kade moved after them as did Blair and Burnie. They felt the danger around the pair and wanted to protect them.

Andy slid to a stop, his eyes on Oshea, not moving towards her. Oshea's arm was grasped tightly in the hand of a man. Andy's face paled as he recognized him.

"Let her go, Littlejohn. She's done nothing to you." Andy's calling out of the man's name branded him in the eyes of the building men.

Davy approached Littlejohn from behind him, not able to get too close just because of the danger to Oshea.

"Not happening. She's coming with me." Littlejohn stood his ground, tightening his grip on Oshea's arm. "No one is stopping me."

He didn't see Bradon moving around to his side that was free, Kade tense beside him, ready to attack the man and bring him down. Only, he had to wait. Oshea was in too much danger at present for him to charge forward and take down the attacker as he had been trained to do.

"Let her go, Littlejohn." Davy's voice behind him startled him, causing him to turn slightly.

"Not happening, cop. She's going with me. She's mine. And he's dead." His free arm swung up, a revolver pointing to Andy.

No one could actually say what happened next, it was all too quick. A slight movement from Bradon's hand and Kade charged forward, his powerful jaws clamping down on Littlejohn's arm and taking him to the ground. His weapon discharged into the ground. Andy had been tackled by Brendon and taken to the ground and safety. Oshea hit hard and then began to kick at Littlejohn while tugging at her arm. Freed, she scrambled to her feet, finding Will there to whisk her off to the building lobby and safety.

Andy was on his feet, running after her, finding her in the middle of the women who had surrounded her. She clung to him, sobs shaking both of their bodies before Will moved them to one of the sitting areas. Fynn and Brady were away and back with water and juice, handing them to the two. Doc appeared, having heard the commotion, and was beside them, asking quick questions and then assessing Oshea's arm.

"It's over?" They could hear the quaver in Oshea's voice. "Is it all over? I hope so. I can't do this any more."

Davy appeared, to crouch down in front of her. He reached for her hands as he prayed for her.

"It's over, Oshea and Andy. He was the last. I must say that he was extremely bold to come on to the Foundation property. But his mindset was that no one could tell him no or stop him."

"Thank God that he is stopped." Andy searched his bride's face. "How many others has he done this to?"

"That we are working through. For now, we want you two and your parents to stay here. We've got some work to do, you two, and need to know that you're safe for now. I'll be back, likely tomorrow." Davy was up and away, walking quickly to meet the patrol officers who had responded.

Chapter 53

Davy was as good as his word, back the next day. But he was not on his own. Oshea turned in the rose garden, Andy beside her, as she heard Davy's voice. She froze, her hands on her face, before she was running. Her parents had appeared with Davy. Her mother's arms went around her as she sobbed, she could feel her father's around the both of them. His prayer reached through her tumbling emotions. Stepping back, Oshea studied her parents.

"Mom? Dad? You're okay?"

"We are, dear." Her mother, Meggie, reached to hug her daughter. "I was horrified to hear what had happened. We were getting letters, supposedly from you, that said you were done with us, that you didn't want anything more to do with us. All we could do was pray."

"Your police detective, Davy, talked to us and told us what had been happening to you. We are so sorry, Oshea. We didn't know that our withdrawal was hurting you. We were just trying to protect you." Her father, Spencer, spoke haltingly.

"I know that now, Dad, but it did hurt. Odell isn't here?"

"No, he's meeting with a detective from another town, he said. He wanted to be here." Spencer looked behind as Andy approached and wrapped her into his arms, drawing her back against her. "And this would be Andy?"

"I am, sir. I am glad to meet you. But I do wish it had been under different circumstances." Andy looked past the older couple to meet Davy's eyes. "Davy?"

"This is enough for the day, Andy. We'll talk more. Call me later this week." Davy walked away, leaving the two couples staring at one another before Andy pointed to the building.

"Let's head in there. There are many people who would like to meet you." He grinned as Oshea dug an elbow into his ribs.

Late that evening, Oshea wandered her home, content now that she knew for certain of Andy's love for her. She had felt it over the last few weeks, but he was consistent now in telling her that. It had also helped to talk with her parents at length. Spencer was still apologizing as they left to return to their home, but one thing was certain for her parents. They were closing down their business, retiring, and moving to Andy's town. Not to keep an eye on them, Meggie said but so that they could get to know one another again. Odell had been in agreement with that.

Andy stood for a moment, his shoulder leaning against his office doorway, just watching his beloved

Oshea. He knew that life would still be difficult but that God had protected them and brought them to one another and that He would be the One leading in their lives. He walked forward, simply wrapping Oshea in his arms and praying for her.

Oshea turned as he did so, content to be held.

"Andy? Did you ever expect to go through what we did?" Oshea drew him to the couch in the office and then cuddled against him.

"Not at all. I looked up that day, saw you, and knew that I could not walk away from you. God was there all the way, sweetheart. And the best part of it all is that you are in my life." Andy kissed her and then rested his chin on her hair.

"Me too. I was so frightened that day. For you as well as me. And angry. And just because of a man who destroyed his own life." Oshea was silent for a few moments. "I spoke with Davy earlier. They're working through all the charges, and there are a lot. He won't tell me what all."

"No, he won't. He can't. But I am sure there are murder charges involved." Andy grew silent, his heart thankful. He looked down and smiled. Oshea had drifted off to sleep. His own eyes grew heavy and he slept too, not feeling the little tuxedo kitten that Oshea had found one day and brought home climbing up to cuddle down with them. Her green eyes blinked as she surveyed her world before a little pink tongue came out to wash at her fur, before she too slept.

Epilogue

Andy was on a search, the little kitten on his shoulder, as he walked through the house. He paused and then nodded. Oshea was likely outside, working in the gardens. She had undertaken the task of revitalizing the gardens, something that he was not aware needed to be done.

Standing near her, Andy's eyes softened as he watched the love of his life just sitting in front of one of the gardens. Empty cell packs from the plants were scattered around and he could see the trowel that she had been using on the grass beside her. The kitten, Kira by name, jumped from his shoulder and raced to climb in her lap, bringing laughter from Oshea.

"Andy? Did you bring Kira out?" Her voice was alive with life and love as she spoke.

"I did. She was riding around on my shoulder again, you know." Andy dropped to a seat beside her, reaching to kiss her, a hand on her cheek. They both began to laugh as Kira protested.

"You're home early, aren't you?" Oshea turned to study the man she loved.

———

"I am. The meeting didn't take as long as Bruce thought, and the weather was good. Now, I'm off until Monday."

"And today is only Thursday." Oshea looked up at him. "That's nice."

"It is. Did Barnabas talk to you?"

"About me being an employee as well? He did. I never expected that."

"No, the ladies didn't but the Board put that in place just to be an encouragement to the couples."

Oshea leaned against him. "They are so thoughtful. The other ladies have talked to me. We're meeting as a group for prayer and Bible study. Fynn has asked if she could meet with me on our own. I think it's wonderful to have so many wonderful Christian friends."

"They are all a wonderful dedicated bunch." Andy finally rose, drawing Oshea to her feet, gathering up the debris from her work in the garden. He had every intention of taking her out for a meal, if she agreed, and he had no doubt that she would.

"Andy?" When he looked at Oshea, he frowned for a moment. "What am I to do? I mean for work?"

"It's up to you. You can do what you want. Your employer wouldn't have to pay you as the Foundation pays you. You can volunteer. You can go back to school or do nothing. That is a choice that we'll discuss and I will back you whatever decision you make."

Oshea moved into his space, hugging him.

———

"God has blessed me with a wonderful, compassionate, caring, Christian husband."

"And me with a wife the same. I love you deeply, Oshea, more than I ever thought I could."

"Did you know that Mom and Dad finally told us where our names came from? From our ancestors. They apparently were embarrassed to tell us."

Andy began to laugh.

"I like that idea, sweetheart. If God blesses us with children, that's something we'll need to consider. A name goes a long way in how people are perceived and treated. We found that out the hard way."

Oshea nodded, her mind already tracking onto something else.

"Andy, what can we do as a couple? I mean as volunteers? I have an idea that I would like to see if we could do."

"And that would be?" Andy waited patiently, knowing that Oshea was still working through what she wanted.

"Something to do with youth. Something that helps to build them up. Something to draw them to their roots and why they are where they are. Does that make sense?" She looked up at him, finding his eyes on her.

"It makes perfect sense. We'll work it through. We can talk to Micah's Kat and she'll gladly help us. For now, though, we set it aside. I want to take you out for dinner."

"You do? We can do that. Only Kira will be lonely." Oshea smirked at him as he laughed at her nonsense, earning herself another kiss.

Thank you for picking up the story of Andy and the love of his life, Oshea. It was my Nanowrimo novel and wrote quickly this time.

A name? We are told a good name is something to be desired. A tarnished name can never be repaired. So what is in your name? I love to look at the meaning of names and see how they fit a person. The characters in my books? Their names are chosen carefully with the meaning something that is definitely chosen for the plot line. I have characters rebel and have needed to choose new names for them.

Andy and Oshea? I never expected the journey that they went on. A dear friend flies and had told me about almost crashing a plane one day. That circumstance I knew would find a way into a book. Andy was the pilot for the Barnabas Foundation and I certainly didn't expect his story to be told. But I could not resist as I saw him standing one day on the sidelines, his eyes on me, just waiting patiently for his story and his lady.

Beloved characters once more appeared in the book. Abe and Emma and their team are found in the

His Guardians series. Doug and Darcy's story is in *The Heart of a Lion* and Dave's is in *A Touch of His Garment*. They always help to move the story forward.

So where do you go from here? A walk with God is never easy, but He is there with us, every step of the way. He does not leave us, does not abandon us. We are called by His name, we are His children.

Andy was a pilot. He was used to flying in different types of weather. That did not stop him. The title of flying high for the king is what we are called to do, no matter where we find ourselves or what circumstances that we're in. We are called to be like the eagles, flying high above the storm. Eagles are one of my favourite birds and I love to see the pictures of them soaring in the sky. That is what I endeavour to try, to soar or fly high for Him.

God bless each one of you as you travel your life's path. Just remember that you are not alone, never alone. God is there with you. He has brought others into your life to walk alongside you. They don't know the path that you walk each day as they walk their own. But their support is there, helping us to make it through each and every day.

Ronna

www.ingramcontent.com/pod-product-compliance
Lightning Source LLC
Chambersburg PA
CBHW061236210726
48293CB00003B/789